DEDICATION

To Sara and Rebecca for being motivational colleagues.
This one is for you.

The Howling Wind
(The Alex Hayden Chronicles Book Two)

MICHAEL ANDREWS

ISBN:150075966X
ISBN-13:978-1500759667

ACKNOWLEDGMENTS

As usual, I have several shout outs to the people who helped me to bring my book to life.
To Rebecca for her wonderful ability to spot all the mistakes that I deliberately put in the drafts. Any mistakes that remain are all of my own making.
To Jessica at Coverbistro for such a great design! Without you, this book would still be sat on my hard drive.

Michael Andrews

Chapter One

"Come on Alex, we'll be late," Harry yelled at me as I fastened up the buttons of the dress shirt that I was being forced into against my will.

"Another minute!" I shouted back as I looked into the mirror. The reflection was almost mocking me as I stared at myself. Dressing up was not something that I enjoyed and when it was for a cause that held little or no meaning to me, it grated even further on my being. I fished out the bowtie and hooked it around my neck, fastening the clip to the side, hidden under the small collar. I had never learned to tie a proper one so Harry and Eirwen had finally given up and bought me a pre-tied one. I picked up the black dinner jacket from the back of the chair and with it hung over my arm, I headed downstairs to meet a similarly dressed Harry.

"You look smart," he smiled at me and reached out to ruffle my hair. I ducked away from him as it had taken me fifteen minutes to style it in the short, spiked style that I had recently started sporting. He laughed and clapped me on the shoulder before we headed out to the elevator to take us down to the underground car park.

"So we are going to this party because?" I left it hanging.

"Because this is a celebration of Vanessa's boss becoming the new Chief Superintendent." He saw my frown. "It means that the post of Superintendent is now vacant,"

"And DCI Bach thinks that she's the woman for the role," I finished for him. My face screwed up. "So we are her back up for her schmoozing up to him in an effort to win favour?"

"She is in a good place at the moment, what with solving the murders," Harry explained as if I was a child. I sighed as I had been involved in political manoeuvring for more years than I cared to remember.

I settled in to the passenger seat of his blue Audi A5 and listened to the sounds of whichever rock band was currently playing on the radio as he drove up the ramp and onto the streets. The party was at the Hilton Hotel which overlooked the beach so we had around a fifteen minute drive to get there. I stared out the window, thinking about the last two months since the encounter with Beddows and Brynhild van Hightinger, and the reappearance of Eirwen, my pretend mother, back into my life.

I had come to Blackpool in my wanderings, hiding from my former sire, Chlothar, and had finally decided that I was too tired to continue running and hiding. I saw the pier in the distance, jutting out into the Irish Sea, I remembered sitting on the end looking over the dark horizon, waiting for the sun to rise and end my existence. That was until Harry Shepherd interrupted me and my life changed in an instant.

Finding out that his son had gone missing eighteen months earlier inspired me to change my mind and with the hunt for the vampire pack, and the subsequent battle with them, a bond of sorts had been formed between us. I knew that he was looking at me as some sort of substitute for Connor, and his insistence of taking care of me brought back long lost memories of my own mother and stepfather, who had passed a millennium before.

I had enlisted the help of Matt, my computer genius partner who had found erased CCTV footage of the night Connor had vanished and to my horror, he had not just run away as was supposed, but he had been approached and seemingly willingly gone with Chlothar, my sire, the one who had turned me a thousand years previously. This weighed heavily on my mind. I had not divulged this information to Harry, or to Eirwen who, like me, was in hiding from our former master.

"We're here," Harry told me, interrupting my thoughts and I grimaced as I saw a long line of people, all suited and booted in their finest, filing into the hotel reception.

"I still don't know why I have to be here," I groused.

"You're supposed to be my nephew for starters, and if Vanessa does get the Superintendent's job, then there is another vacancy coming up," he grinned as I shook my head. "Secondly, you've been getting moody over the last couple of weeks and I thought a party might cheer you up."

"I've not been moody," I shot back, sounding exactly like the moody teenager that he was claiming I was, before chuckling to myself at the absurdity of my statement.

"And thirdly," he paused, flashing a look of worried concern at me. "Bill told me that Petra is coming back to visit for a week."

"Oh that's just bloody marvellous!" I hissed. "She'd better have gotten an attitude improvement." The image of the sixteen year old blonde sprang to mind with mixed emotions attached to it. She was an attractive girl for sure, the way that her green eyes sparkled when she was enthusiastic about a subject. Unfortunately for me, that subject seemed to be the various ways that she wished to end my existence. While she was a skilled fighter, I was confident in my ability to remain better than her, unless she got her crossbow out. The shots that she had fired off in the Church of the Merciful Heart certainly showed prowess that I hadn't seen for centuries.

"Just let her get settled in to Bill's before you two go head to head again, will you?"

"I'd be perfectly happy to avoid her altogether but I doubt that's going to happen, is it?"

I saw Harry slowly shake his head. Since being exposed to the supernatural world that existed around him, he had become firm friends with his neighbour Bill, something that despite our reluctant alliance those months ago, still rankled with me. After all, can you imagine what it is like living next to a born killer who is ready to wipe out your entire race if the order came down from The Comitia?

The Comitia. How my body had shivered when I found out that they were the ones who had sent Petra to help her uncle. They were the ruling body of humans who reluctantly accepted the existence of my kind with open arms while in the background, were plotting ways of ridding the Earth of all paranormal creatures. It didn't matter that some of us actually helped humans to grow and progress, pouring money and brains into projects, while humans seemed bent on destroying the natural world around them.

I pushed the door open and stepped out, putting my jacket on and fastening the buttons while I waited for Harry to do the same. We walked over to the reception, the picture of a normal family, well, an uncle and nephew anyway.

"HARRY!" the loud shout of Detective Sam Jackson echoed over the buzz of conversation of the people in line.

"Hey Sammy," Harry shook the offered hand of his partner.

"Hi Detective Jackson," I smiled at him. "How's your wife?"

"Oh, she's fine and so is little Samuel Junior," he replied, his chest puffing out proudly. "You must come round sometime and see the little blighter."

"Is he still screaming the house down?" I asked. The last thing that I needed was to be anywhere near a two week old baby when it started wailing. Even with the ability to turn off my higher strength hearing, crying babies did nothing for me.

"Unfortunately yes," he frowned. "And I have no idea how a baby that small can produce so much shi… ah, pooh."

I chuckled at his scrunched up nose, my own mirroring it at the imagined stench of a dirty nappy. We filed past the waiting crowd, Harry and Sam's status of detectives enough to bump us through. We made it into the large function room that was decorated in a mixture of the black of the police and the bright orange of the new Chief Superintendent Greg Leighton's favourite football team. Loud music played through speakers and I could quickly count over a hundred people already inside. Guessing that the figure would double by the time that everyone was inside, I tried to sneak off to the side before a firm hand clapped on my shoulder.

"Oh no you don't! If I have to endure this, then so do you!" I looked up into the faked smile of the tall figure of Eirwen, my fellow vampire and former mother figure. Now that she was confident that she was under the protection of The Council of Vampires, she had allowed her hair to grow back into her normal platinum blonde instead of the dyed black while she was in hiding. Dressed in a gown of pure gold, she looked stunning.

"I see you're keeping a low profile, mother," I sniggered.

"It's not very often that I get to party, so why not?" she replied. "You never know, I might even get lucky."

"Yuck!" I made a gagging motion. "You're my mother! I'm not supposed to have thoughts like that about you."

"It's just a shame that you were turned so young," she cupped my face. "Another three or four years and you would have the girls fighting for you, especially that Petra girl."

"Oh puh-lease!" I scowled. "She hates our kind with a venom. If I was in bed with her, she'd likely stab me through the heart while I slept."

"So is Uncle Harry here?"

"Over at the bar with Jackson. What about Vanessa?"

"She's talking with CS Leighton and Commissioner Edwards somewhere. Let's get a drink and then go and socialise."

She left me no choice but to follow as she took my hand and half dragged me to the bar. Despite wanting to try to blind the night with alcohol, I knew that with so many police in attendance, the likelihood of getting served was nil so I spent the next three and a half hours being tortured in a manner far worse than those of medieval times. After all, there are only so many times that your cheeks can cope with being pinched by women in their fifties or older, your shoulder being clapped by the strong arms of law enforcers and only so many times you can avoid the attention of the mob of teenage girls who found themselves in attendance, their evening entertainment now focused on trying to capture me into a dance.

Finally, with CS Leighton making his speech of appreciation for everyone attending, I found myself outside in the cool, midnight air. I could hear the faint lapping of the waves and as I leaned against a planted palm tree, I allowed myself to relax and calm my body from the on edge state that it had been in.

As my body became in tune with my surroundings, I felt a wrongness. I kept my eyes closed as I opened my mind, casting my empathic sensors about to see if I could locate the source of the feeling.

"There you are," the slightly slurred voice of Detective Jackson interrupted my search. "Harry is looking for you."

"Is he ready to go?" I asked hopefully.

"I think so," he hiccupped, just as Harry appeared over his shoulder. I jumped back as I felt the change in Jackson's body and vacated the spot where he emptied the eight shots of Sambuca and god knows what else onto the floor.

"Let me call you a taxi, Sam," Harry said, taking his car keys from him. He fished out his mobile and as I half listened to him speak with the taxi company, the hairs on the back of my neck prickled. I looked around again but could only see people milling around, trying to remember where they had parked their cars or waiting for taxis, just like Sam would have to.

My eyes fell onto a family of four whom I had seen earlier. They had mainly kept to themselves during the party, although the daughter, who looked to be around sixteen, had given me a few discrete smiles. I blushed as her eyes now caught mine, her brown eyes like dark chocolate pools but as she brushed a strand of her brown hair from her face, I saw her father say something in her ear. She stiffened immediately and looked down at the ground. I didn't need my empathic senses to feel the anger flowing from him and when he caught my gaze, there was a look of hatred in his eyes that made me shiver. I wondered who this man was and what he had encountered to make him have such hatred like that. "Who are they?" I asked as DCI Bach appeared by our side.

"That's Ian Norris and his family," she replied after noticing who I was asking about. "Last month, he relocated his electronics company to the town, which is great news as it has created around two hundred jobs in the area."

Any further conversation was cut short as a taxi pulled up and Eirwen and Vanessa offered to make sure that Jackson got home safely. How safe he would be once he got home was another question, as surely his wife would have something to say about the state that he had gotten into.

I looked back over to where the Norris's had been stood but they had disappeared, either into their car or a taxi of their own. A blonde figure was stood in their place however, one that I now figured to be the cause of my earlier feeling.

"Oh for Christ's sake," I hissed, causing Harry to look at me.

"What's wrong?"

"It's not my fault, okay?"

"What isn't?"

"Hello Detective Shepherd," the sweet, clear voice of the sixteen year old girl announced her presence.

"Oh. Hello Petra. I thought you'd be at your uncle's?"

"I thought that I'd do a quick scout around, just to see if there have been any changes." Petra Farrelly replied. She gave me a once over look. "Well, it isn't true what they say."

"And what might that be?" I sighed.

"You can scrub scum up." She smiled at me. "You actually look quite good in that. One might even forget what you are."

"Thanks, I think."

"But just remember, I won't forget."

"I wouldn't expect you to."

"Okay, knock it off the pair of you. We'll have no fighting here. Save it for a practice mat," Harry scolded us. "Are you okay to get home or do you want a lift?"

"I'll have a lift thanks." Petra replied. "But I call shotgun."

"Don't," was all Harry said to me as I bristled to retort. "Just get in the back please, Alex."

I bit my lip and got in behind Harry, not giving Petra the pleasure of being the person to be sitting in front of me. I pretended not to be listening as Harry asked her how she had been and she told him about the new training that she had undertaken after leaving Blackpool. Shaking my head, I settled down for the short ride home, pleased when I finally got back to my room and shed my suit. Even though it was still early and I didn't need any rest, I climbed into the four poster bed and drew the drapes around it. I lay on the bed and, for the next two hours, thought about police politics, the strange behaviour of the Norris's and finally, how the return of the sixteen year old hunter would change the atmosphere of the neighbourhood.

Michael Andrews

Chapter Two

I awoke to the smell of coffee, drifting through the drapes of my bed. My pretend uncle had got me hooked on the damn stuff over the last month and I now looked forward to my wake up mug of strong, black coffee. Pulling the drapes back, I quickly drained the cup before getting myself ready and heading downstairs.

I wasn't surprised to see Bill sitting at the kitchen table, as the old hunter was a regular visitor to Harry's house, making sure that he was settling into the new world that he had become embroiled into. However, my stomach took an unpleasant turn when the blonde hair of Petra came into view as I walked into the kitchen. I nodded at Bill, said a brief greeting to Harry and ignored the girl as I washed up my cup in the sink.

"So, what's your plan for this evening, Alex?" Harry queried.

"I thought I'd have a fly about, grab a virgin and slaughter her while feasting on her blood before dumping her body in the sea," I smiled back. I didn't need my skills to sense Petra's pose stiffen immediately.

"He's kidding, Petra," Bill chuckled, knowing of the antagonism that existed between the pair of us. I flashed him a grin that reassured him that I was.

"I am going to go on a fly around though, just to sweep the area," I told them. "It's been too quiet around here and that doesn't sit well with me."

"Well, maybe killing off those vampires has sent a warning out that we're not to be messed with." Petra remarked, pride in her voice at her part in the fight.

"It will have sent out a message, but one that told Eirik van Hightinger exactly where Eirwen and I are living," I frowned. "I was expecting some type of retaliation by now."

"If the Council are protecting Eirwen like she says they are, maybe they've warned him off?" Bill posed.

"Eirik is not someone who takes much notice of the Council, and Brynhild certainly will ignore anything that they say."

"Why don't you take Petra out with you so that she can get some experience in what you are looking for?" Harry suggested.

"I don't think so," I snapped and turned quickly, walking into the lounge to get my trainers. I could hear Bill and Petra arguing and for once, I sided with the young hunter. There was no way that she and I were going to become friends, so the idea of teaching her skills that ultimately she could use against me was not something that I was willingly going to do.

"It was just an idea," Harry said, making me jump. Not for the first time, he had managed to walk up on me without my knowledge, something that I was going to have to look into. My mind had always alerted me to anyone who approached me, but somehow the detective continually evaded my defence.

"I know that you want us to be pally pally, but it isn't going to happen," I told him. "I'm going to go and have a cruise about and I'll pop into the station later."

"Be careful out there," he replied but before he could pat me on the shoulder or anything, I was up and gone, speeding through the door and into the air.

I struggled at first to get any height as a bitter cold wind blew in from the Irish Sea, but finally finding a slightly warmer air current, I glided up to a height of a few hundred feet, far enough from the ground that it would be impossible for a human to see me. Dressed all in black, I didn't need my glimmer glyph which was pleasing as I could concentrate on searching the streets of Blackpool.

After agreeing to stay, I had first thought about becoming a Batman-like figure, searching out criminals and bringing them to a swift justice, until Eirwen pointed out that I would start to attract the attention of the media if I did. My childish dreams of heroism faded so I settled for texting Harry with any major crimes that were taking place while keeping a sweep going for anything non-human. It was my one concession to him so far, allowing him to get me a mobile phone.

Tonight was looking like it was no different to the others. I landed quietly in a darkened alley behind the main promenade and walked around the corner. With winter now in full swing, darkness came early to northern England so not many businesses were still open. Most of the holiday season businesses had closed down for the winter period but there were still a couple of the arcades open so I decided to amuse myself on my favourite zombie killing shoot 'em up. However, as I walked in, I frowned to myself as I could see that it was already occupied by a dark haired kid who looked to be a couple of years younger than my own appearance.

I walked over to the change machine, pushing in a twenty and getting the necessary amount of pound coins in exchange. I nodded at the middle aged woman who worked the concessions counter, flashing her one of my killer smiles that I knew softened her heart towards me. A quick smile and a polite manner always worked well with the staff who allowed me to stay beyond what they would any other under-aged kid without them looking to call my parents. Moving behind the young lad, I could see that he was putting in a decent performance, killing the rampant zombie army, but as his character succumbed to the flesh eating monsters, he let loose with a string of curses that would have made even Eirwen blush.

"Hey, you're pretty good at this," I said as way of greeting.

"Nah, I'm okay but looks like someone from here is awesome. Look at that top score!" The lad turned towards me and I stood stock still as I recognised his face from the party the previous evening. Deciding that I wanted to find out a little more about him, I pulled out a couple of coins.

"Do you fancy pairing up?" I asked. "There's a two player option."

"Sure," he smiled. "I could use some help. Didn't I see you last night at that party for that policeman?"

"Yeah, I was dragged there by my uncle," I played it cool. "I'm Alex."

"Jake." He offered me his fist and having watched a few American films recently, I rolled up my own and bumped it in greeting. "My Dad told me that we had to go as well. He knows him through his business or something." We put in the money and the game started up. I decided to play it cool, allowing Jake to take the lead rather than showing off my supernatural reactions and before I knew it, we were already on the tenth level with only a loss of three lives.

"So you're pretty good at this," Jake said, breaking my concentration. "I mean, I can tell you're holding back."

"What do you mean? You've got a higher score than me," I pointed out.

"Yeah but you're not taking the shots that you could. When you need to though, you nail every shot."

BUSTED!

"I guess I've just had more practice than you," I offered, "This is my favourite game in here."

"I can relate to that," he sniggered. "Nothing like killing zombies is there?"

I paused to look at him, wondering if there was a hidden meaning in his words. However, his face reflected his enthusiasm for the game, so I just put it down to the thirteen year old boyish enjoyment that I'm sure it was.

"So when did your family move here?" I asked as we walked over to the concessions counter. "I heard that your dad is like some big owner of a company."

"Urgh," he pulled a face. "We moved here last month 'cos my Dad decided he wanted to move the company here as the cost of wages is less, and people will be more willing to work for lower wages as they'd be happy just to get a job."

"Sounds a bit mercenary," I chuckled. "But totally right from a business point of view."

"I guess so, but Blackpool? Why couldn't we have gone to Manchester or Liverpool or somewhere less, um," he paused.

"Less run down?" He nodded. "It's okay here, especially during the summer. It kind of all closes down in the winter as most people come here for the touristy shit."

"I'll trust you on that," he grunted. "As I said, my Dad knows that copper from somewhere and it was Mr Leighton who persuaded Dad to come here. Something about paying less tax or something as well."

I heard a low bleep and buzz and looked around, only to see Jake pulling a mobile from his jeans pocket. He frowned as he read the text message and as much as I wanted to sneak a peak, I decided to respect his privacy. After all, Harry and Eirwen had tried to impress on me the need to look like I was actually Harry's nephew, and a fourteen year old lad, so making a friend of sorts would help.

"I'm sorry Alex, but I've gotta shoot," Jake sighed. "My Mother has told me that I need to get home."

"No problem buddy," I reassured him. "My uncle can be a bit overbearing at times as well."

"Will you be here tomorrow?" He had a look of a little lost puppy and I guessed that being the son of a rich businessman had its drawbacks. He had told me in our small talk that his sister and he were being home-schooled so I nodded and agreed to meet him around the same time the following day. He beamed a smile at me and, with another fist bump, left the arcade.

I wandered down towards the end of the pier and took up my customary seat on the end, wanting to enjoy a little peace and quiet to ponder but that was soon interrupted. With a soft sigh, I waited for her to talk.

"So it looks like you've made a new friend, or is he your next meal?"

"I thought that we had agreed to avoid each other Petra?" I asked without turning.

"I know it's only going to be a matter of time before you start killing again, no matter what Uncle Bill says," she snarled. "You're all the same, you blood suckers. You kill without mercy or conscience and think you're above the law."

If she was going to insult me any further, she didn't get a chance as with a burst of speed and anger, I pinned her against the side of a closed down café that was some forty metres from where I had been sitting. I could feel my eyes turning red as my animalistic nature fought to take control. I held her still, my fingers slowly tightening around her throat before I stopped myself from strangling the life from her. Letting her go, she dropped to the ground, gasping for air and I looked her in the eyes, my fangs fully bared.

"Do not think for one minute that if I or mine are threatened in any way, I will not react with the full fury of my arsenal," I hissed at her, making her shrink back against the wall. The look of fear was evident in her bright green eyes and I fought to control myself, to bring myself back to human form. "You are correct in that all vampires are capable of killing at will as individually, humans do not have the ability to fight us. However, not all vampires choose to kill at will. Some show respect and restraint for humanity, and it would be nice if that was reciprocated every now and then."

I didn't wait for a reply but launched myself from the end of the pier, snagging a blast of warm air and headed over to the police station where Harry was stationed. Landing on my tiptoes in the deserted street next to the station, I slowly counted to ten to try to diffuse my anger, which was aimed more at myself rather than at Bill's niece. How I managed to let her get under my skin so often was beyond me.

Walking into the station, I nodded a hello to the desk sergeant on duty, all of whom were now used to seeing me, and I wandered through into the office where Harry and the others were based. I looked around, surprised to see it empty so I let my senses take over.

"There's nothing to indicate that this is anything other than an animal attack," I heard DCI Bach's voice echoing from the conference room nearby. "But after those murders of the women a couple of months ago, the Mayor and the new Chief Superintendent are both very twitchy and want us to check it out."

"But why the whole department, ma'am?" a new voice asked. "Surely if it is just some hikers who got attacked, then only one or two detectives need to look into it."

"We just need to cover all bases, and be seen that we take any investigation seriously," Harry piped up. "The flack that we got over the murders was unbelievable so it's more about PR than anything else."

There were a few disgruntled murmurs before the scraping of chair legs indicated that the meeting was over. I took a seat in Harry's chair, idly doodling on a scrap of paper when the eight strong detective team filed back into the office. Most recognised my presence with a nod, although Detective Jackson was still looking green around the gills as he sat down opposite me.

"Alex, you're back," Harry greeted me. "Find anything?"

"Not really," I sighed. "I bumped into Petra while I was out, so you may get some grief off her uncle when you get back."

"How much did you hurt her?" he groaned.

I smiled and shrugged before picking up the folder that he had just placed on the desk. I flicked through it, scanning the photos of white bones, some of which still had decomposing flesh attached to them. The report listed them as three John Doe's and a Jane Doe, but from the size of some of the bones, it would be a good guess that they were a family, or at least there were two adults and two children.

"So where were these found?" I asked, looking for something to pass the time.

"Eh? Oh, the bodies. Over in the woods at Marton Mere," Jackson grunted. Seeing my questioning look, he continued. "It's a local nature reserve out by the golf club. It's a popular spot for walkers as there's a reservoir and some woodlands."

"Any clue who they are?"

"Not yet. Doctor Stirling has run the DNA but there's no match," Harry replied. "But then again, we only carry records of criminals, so it's unsurprising."

I raised my eyebrows at his statement, which caused him to give me a questioning look.

"Really? You believe that?" I shook my head. Turning his monitor on, I pulled up a blank internet screen. My fingers blurred as I keyed into the secret database that nobody outside of certain agencies were supposed to know about, and by cross checking the now hacked records of Doctor Stirling with the information on the database, I printed off the details of the dead family. I motioned for him to follow me into DCI Bach's office where I handed Harry the printout.

"Leo Varsey, forty three, resident of Staines, Middlesex went on holiday five weeks ago and failed to return to work. His wife, Fran, also forty three and their sons Vincent, fourteen and Adrian, thirteen also were reported by their school to have failed to return," Harry read. "Letters were sent three weeks ago to the schools and employers stating that there had been a family emergency in Italy and that they were relocating before a car crash just south of Milan killed all four."

"But Dr Stirling put the deaths at thirty two days ago," Harry argued.

"What's this?" DCI Bach asked.

"It looks like there's been a cover up somewhere to hide the fact that these people are dead," I explained. "There are only two scenarios why this would occur."

"Either the family were not who they seemed and were non-human," the DCI started.

"Or they were killed by something not human, and I don't mean the beast of bloody Bodmin Moor!" I finished.

"Maybe Eirwen and you should go and look at the remains," she suggested.

"Can you swing that without the Doctor's approval?" Harry asked her. "If I remember rightly, he was getting a little close to the truth about the murders."

"Pfah!" I chuckled. "We don't need the good Doctor's permission to get in."

"Well, whatever you do, it will have to wait," DCI Bach told me. "It's sun rise soon and you won't get in and out before it's up."

"God! Firstly I've got Eirwen telling me what to do and now you're acting like my mother as well!" I grumbled.

I turned and left the office, ignoring the smiles on Harry's and Vanessa's faces before jumping into the air to take to wing.

Chapter Three

Moonlight shone through the canopy of the forest as I crept on quiet feet, avoiding the loose twigs on the grassy floor. My nose picked up the scent of my prey, the smell of damp fur lingering in the air as I grew ever closer. My own coat of black fur was dry, as I had sensed the sudden downpour coming and had transformed into a bat and had ridden out the twenty minute drenching in the safety of a hollowed out tree.

As I prowled forwards, crouching low to the ground, I sensed a sudden change within the nature of the forest. My hackles stood on edge and I froze, no longer the confident varg but one that recognised danger.

I sensed, rather than heard, the soft landing behind me but as I turned, my fangs bared to attack, I pulled back as I saw the commanding figure of Captain Paulinos du Balurac. I transformed back in an instant, knowing that there was something wrong if he had ended my varg training in such a fashion.

"Captain, what's wrong?" I asked.

"Hush boy," he chided me. I bristled as it still rankled me that it had been three hundred years since my conversion and he still called me boy.

"Why have we stopped?" I whispered, keeping my voice so low that only a vampire could hear.

"We have company," the tall, dark figure replied. "And it isn't friendly."

"Another vampire?" My body shivered in anticipation. For the last two hundred years, ever since my powers had started to manifest, Chlothar had instructed the Captain to take charge of my training. I could already best most within the House of Chlothar, but I had yet to meet another vampire in a serious confrontation. The adrenaline started to pump through my body as I could feel myself giving over to the change.

"Not now, Alexander," Paulinos snapped at me. "This is no vampire. Quickly, up here!"

He grabbed me by the scruff of my collar and with a powerful leap, we were perched on a high branch some eighty metres above the ground. I calmed my heart down, allowing my body to return to normal. The last thing that I wanted to do was upset the Captain, who after delivering his own punishment to me, normally in the form of a physical fight with him, he would hand me over to our sire for further discipline.

We crouched motionless on the tree limb, an eerie silence having fallen over the woods. Even the night owls were quiet and the nocturnal rodents hidden away. Finally my blossoming enhanced hearing picked up the soft pad-pad of paw steps on the grassy carpet of the wood. Deep, heavy breathing accompanied it before a hiss of pure hatred almost made me lose my balance. Turning to look at the Captain, I was shocked to see him in full blown vampire transformation.

"Stay here, Alexander," he instructed me. "If I do not return forthwith, fly back to the castle and inform our sire that Kiran Gestarde has returned to our range."

"Who?" I asked to empty space as Captain Paulinos dropped gracefully to the floor. His speed surprised me as he blurred from my vision, the rustle of leaves the only sign of his passing.

I waited on the branch, not moving, not daring to move. I could hear the sounds of a scuffle; a fight. My heart started to pump faster as the grunts of pain and the smell of fresh blood assailed my senses. My fangs began to extend as my vampire nature called out for me to forgo the instructions of my teacher and join him in battle against the unknown enemy.

A howl of pain unlike anything I had ever heard before broke the silence, sending the rodents scurrying from their hideaways and owls took to wing to escape the unnatural confrontation that was taking place close by.

I was ready. My fingernails had extended into the claws that I used to fight with, my vision flicking between infrared and normal as my growing powers battled to aid me. I was about to disobey my Captain when a pitiful yelp of agony deafened me. The pitch was beyond normal human hearing but to a vampire, it rattled my brain. Clutching at my ears, trying to cover them, I rocked back and forth, trying to block out the pain. I could feel myself beginning to lose consciousness and with a leap, I threw myself into the air to try to escape the range of the cry.

I hit the ground hard, unable to catch an air current with my inability to focus my concentration and I lay on the grass, gasping for breath, my lungs sucking in replacement air after my winding. I heard heavy footsteps approaching but as I tried to roll over to find a hiding place, a hand touched my shoulder.

"It's okay Alexander, you're safe," Captain Paulinos told me. I looked up at his bloodied chainmail shirt. His mouth was a mess of fur and blood but there was an exultant look burning in his eyes. "Come, let me show you our enemy."

I jerked awake with my fangs bared, my heart pumping in my chest. Darkness surrounded me, but my night vision easily outlined the drapes of my four poster bed, and the bedroom beyond them. Sitting upright, I counted to ten while I calmed my breathing. Sweat trickled down my brow, which I wiped away with the back of my hand.

"I thought I'd stopped having these damned dreams!" I groaned to myself. Ever since the death of Beddows van Hightinger, my sleep had been dreamless. The thought that Chlothar had been in this very house played on my mind, but the nightmares that I had been having had long since disappeared.

I pulled back the drapes and fired up the computer. I logged on using a secondary account that I had created, just on the off chance that Harry ever came in while I was just browsing the internet. I'd set this account up to continue my search for Connor, and for my sire.

I re-watched the video clip that Matt had sent me, looking for something, anything that suggested Connor had been taken against his will. However each time that I watched it, I grew more convinced that not only had he gone willingly, but that he had somehow known that the three vampires would visit him that night.

Looking at the timestamp on the video clip, it was now some twenty months since Connor Shepherd had left. My initial thought that he would be long dead had been replaced with the cold knowledge that he would now be a vampire, an undead creature and one of my sire's household.

With the aid of a programme that Matt had designed, I set my laptop running yet another search for the location of my former master. My initial enquiries had found that I was correct in that Chlothar had left the castle in Northern France but I was having a distinct lack of success in tracing him after the household had moved to Canada.

Flicking the screen saver on, knowing that the encryption programme would defy anyone other than Matt, or maybe the NSA's best cyber hacker, I pulled on a fresh set of clothes and headed downstairs. I paused in the hallway, sighing inwardly as I sensed the presence of both Bill and Petra, but at least I would have some backup.

"Mother! So nice to see you," I smiled as Eirwen allowed me to hug her tightly. Putting on the show of family affection seemed to settle Bill down but I could feel the daggers penetrating my back as the steely glare of the young blonde bore into my back. "Uncle Harry, how are you today?"

"Okay, why are you playing the idiot?" he chuckled.

"Well, you want me to act like your fourteen year old nephew so I thought I'd get some practice in," I smiled sweetly. "Hey, I can turn on the charm when needed. It's what makes me so dangerous." I heard Petra's grunt and I flashed her a knowing look. I could see faint bruising around her neck, but for once, chose not to apologise for my outburst.

"I hear you made a friend last night," Harry said. "Just be careful that he doesn't want you to go off playing football in the day or something."

"You could always play in skins while you do," Petra added, a grin on her face as we both knew it wasn't seeing me shirtless that she was really interested in.

"Does every evening start like this, Detective Shepherd?" Eirwen asked, a frown on her face.

"Only the ones when both of the children are in the room," Bill laughed. Both Petra and I shot him a withering look, something that we could both agree on was being insulted at being called children.

"What are you doing here anyway, Eirwen?" I asked.

"Vanessa suggested that we go and take a look at the remains of the bodies. No time like the present."

"I'm in," I quickly agreed. The less time spent with Petra was the less time that I was thinking about killing her.

"I'll give you a call at the station when we're done and we can meet at the café to discuss our findings," Eirwen told my new uncle. "You two as well," she said to the two hunters.

I groaned and led the way out of the kitchen, through the lounge, out of the door and threw myself into the air. Eirwen was soon alongside me, although I did have to slow down occasionally as my speed had always been quicker than hers. It didn't take many minutes before we were landing on the roof of the hospital where Doctor Stirling was based.

Unlike most buildings in England, the hospital actually did have roof access, mainly to allow any incoming air ambulances to land and transport their patients quickly inside to get treatment. I tested the door and found it open. After all, how many burglars would scale the five stories to get to the roof when they could simply walk in through the front door?

"The morgue is on the ground floor," Eirwen told me as I pulled the door open.

"So why didn't we go through the front door?" I complained.

"I can't glimmer like you can," she frowned at me. "I've never been able to master that trick."

"Come on, let's go," I shrugged. It wasn't my fault, after all. I had spent forty years trying to teach her the trick, but her sub-conscious just wouldn't let her fade into the background. Something to do with how beautiful she was, I suppose.

We crept through the deserted corridors, the night staff only interested in sitting at their stations, reading or surfing the internet while their patients slept. As we found the thick steel doors that had the words 'Morgue' written on in deep red paint, something that I thought was a little morbid, I felt the coldness already seeping out of the room.

With a slight shiver, I pulled the door open and we stepped inside. Immediately the smell of dead flesh assailed us, making me gag slightly but as my eyes scanned the room, I saw the bones of the four bodies set out on the cold metal tables.

As the records had shown, they were the bones of an adult male and female, along with those of two teenage boys. Any flesh that had remained on the bones had been removed, much to my annoyance but as Eirwen silently handed me the fibula of the father, Leo, a low growl erupted from my mouth.

"Are these marks on all four?" I gritted my teeth as I ran my finger over the deep gouges in the bone.

"There are some on the hip bone of the female, while I can see scratches on the ribs and spines of the boys," she replied, sadness in her voice.

"I guess that answers the question of which of the two reasons why the deaths have been covered up." I put the leg bone back in place before looking at the remains of Vincent Varsey. He looked to have been the same height as me, and with his younger, smaller brother by his side, the pair of small humans would not have stood a chance against their killer.

"Look at this, Alexander," Eirwen interrupted my thoughts. "These are not the same teeth marks."

I looked at the bones that she was indicating and sure enough, there were different sized bite marks on them.

"Maybe it was just some of the animals escaped from the zoo?" I asked hopefully.

"Nothing has been reported, and before you ask," she smiled at me, knowing that I would, "the director is a close friend and he would have told me if there had been an escape. I've helped him get some previous escapees back before they could cause any damaged."

"Is he bonded as well?" I frowned at her. "You can't keep bonding, you know. You can only have so many linked at one time."

"I know the rules as well as you do," she snapped at me. "The director is Vanessa's brother in law, Jason's adopted father."

"Oh. That's okay then," I apologised. "I guess that explains why Jason loves the zoo."

"So if it's not an escaped animal, and there are more than one…" Eirwen left it hanging.

"Then we have a huge problem," I finished for her.

Chapter Four

"Coffee?" Harry asked as I sat down heavily on the empty seat next to him.

"Please," I replied. "And ask Edna to put a double whisky in it as well."

"That bad?" Bill asked, his face showing concern.

"It looks like it," Eirwen sighed, her pale features looking drawn in worry.

"What did you find out?" Harry queried, returning with a mug of black liquid. I took a sip, my eyes flashing to his as I tasted only coffee. "You're still underage, remember."

"Oh for crying out loud," I complained before hearing a snigger from Petra. "We'll need to do some more scouting around, but the bones were showing all of the signs of a werewolf attack."

"WEREWOLF?" the blonde gasped out. "No way! Not here!"

"Why not here?" DCI Bach asked. "After all, they are humans for most of the month, aren't they?"

"If you want to call them human, you can do," I hissed. "There are other names that I'd prefer to call them."

"Them?" Bill picked up. "You think that there is a pack?"

"We found differing sizes of bite marks, which indicates that there are at least three, if not four lycans that were involved in the attack," Eirwen explained.

"So how do we know if they are still here?" Petra asked, a nervousness to her voice that I had not heard before. I looked over at her and her face was so white that she looked to be on the point of fainting. I bit back the sarcastic tone that normally sprung to my lips whenever we were involved in a conversation.

"Unfortunately, while they are in human form, it's difficult to tell them apart from normal humans," I replied. "Once the moon starts to wax into fullness, there should be signs of differing behaviour as the lycan nature starts to come through."

"So can we catch them before the full moon hits and they kill again?" the old hunter asked. "I've not got much experience with the wolves," he explained. "We don't get to see many of them in England."

"If we can spot them and trap them, then we can cage them before they turn fully," Eirwen stroked his hand fondly.

"Or we can kill them on the spot," I added.

"Can they be cured?" Harry asked. "I've read books where the pack changes back if you kill the alpha dog, or whatever it's called."

"That's just a rumour," Eirwen said sadly. "We've never seen it happen, but that isn't to say it isn't true."

"So what now?" Petra queried.

"We step up our scouting, and keep our eyes peeled," Eirwen replied. "There are two days until the next full moon and if they are still here, they will attack again."

"Why?" Harry asked. "What makes them attack? I mean, if they are mostly human, then they can eat normally can't they?"

"It's in their nature to kill," I told them, answering Harry's question. "They are territorial and feel that they have to lay down markers to their range."

"So the question is, do we know of anyone who has moved here recently, or are they just passing through?" Bill asked, looking at DCI Bach.

"Are you seriously asking me that question?" she sighed. "We get around ten million tourists a year, not to mention business conventions and the like."

"Hold on a second," I jumped. "Didn't you say that Ian Norris moved here about a month ago?"

"So?"

"Eirwen thinks that there could be four of the beasts in the pack," I pointed out. "That's him, his wife, Sarah Louise and Jake."

"Oh no you don't," Eirwen started. "You don't get out of making a friend that easily."

"What?"

"You want us to believe that the lad is a werewolf just so you have a reason to going back to being all moody again," my mother scolded me, catching me unaware.

I thought for a moment. Was my automatic self-defence bringing in excuses to re-raise the barrier of my lonely existence of the previous one hundred and fifty years? I had lowered it over the last couple of months, allowing first Harry, and now the others inside. I shrugged it off.

"Well, I'm going to keep an eye on them anyway," I huffed at the slight that Eirwen had cast on my reasoning, getting up and leaving them sitting in the café as I stepped outside into the road opposite the pier.

Cruising the airways had always calmed me down. There is a sense of peacefulness in the night air with no chattering birds to distract you but, as I landed on top of the Tower, perching myself easily on the outside ledge, I found my mind wandering.

Was I really that worried about making friends once again that I would look for any reason to distance myself from a human? I remembered the heartache that I felt with the death of Geraff, the serf boy killed by Bradlow van

Hightinger. There had been several occasions when a girl had caught my eye throughout the centuries, only for her to run screaming into the distance once my true nature was revealed to her; or the two occasions where Chlothar had refused to turn the object of my affection. In both instances, the girl in question was ruthlessly slaughtered by Captain Paulinos, putting me back in my place within the household.

My eyes scanned the sea front street, watching the thinning crowds of tourists aimlessly wandering from bar to bar, nightclub to nightclub, all in search of their next drink. It was mainly stag and hen parties, with the holiday season now closed down, although with the Christmas celebrations just around the corner, the famous Blackpool Illuminations did attract their fair share of families.

I felt a pull towards the street, just off the main street and deciding to go with my feelings, I dropped myself down onto the roof of a nearby shop before scaling down the drainpipe. Walking out of the small side street, I found myself next to the amusement arcade where I had met up with Jake Norris the evening before. Sure enough, he was back in the arcade, the promise that I had made to him about meeting up coming back to my mind.

I watched him for a few minutes, looking for the signs that would mark him as a lycan, but as he played on the zombie shoot 'em up, all I saw was a thirteen year boy enjoying himself. Well, as much as a thirteen year old can enjoy himself whilst being killed by zombies.

"For feck's sake," I heard him curse. "Stop killing me you tossers!"

"Feck?" I chuckled as I approached him. He turned and a smile lit up his face as I handed him a can of soda. "There are other words that I would use if I was being eaten alive by zombies."

"Alex! You came!" he grinned. "I thought that you had bailed on me, or that I'd got the time wrong or something."

"No, it's me being late, sorry," I apologised. "My uncle kept me late meeting some friends of his."

"Well, you're here now," the brown haired lad patted my arm. "Let's kill some zombies!"

That always sounded good to me, zombie killing, so it was with some pleasure that I spent the next hour playing the game with him, shooting the flesh eating monsters before they could kill us. As the levels progressively got more difficult, the banter between us got louder as we laughed our way to the point where Jake told me that he had to stop before he had an accident.

"Well, that wouldn't be nice, would it," a deep voice behind us interrupted. "Play time is over for you little pussies. Shift it before we get annoyed."

We both turned and found ourselves face to face with four guys who looked to be in their early twenties. All four were dressed in a poor imitation of a gang, ripped jeans, dark shirts and black leather jackets that had seen better times. They all had sneers on their faces as if they were supposed to be intimidating.

"Yeah, sure," Jake stuttered out, a look of fear in his eyes as he took in the appearance of the youths.

"No, we're not finished yet," I complained. "We've still got six credits in." I looked over the thugs and knew that they would be no match for me.

"Let's go, Alex," my new friend tugged my arm. "It's not worth getting beat up or anything."

"Listen to your mate, kid," the obvious leader of the four grinned at me. "You don't wanna mess with us."

I bit my tongue as two of the larger youths flexed their arms in an attempt to show off their muscles, as if that was going to scare me. I flashed a look over at Jake and could see him trying to edge away but the gang must have decided that I had taken too long to move. I was caught slightly off guard as the nearest thug pushed me back into the game console but as I felt the adrenaline begin to rush through me, another punched Jake in the stomach.

I heard his groan of pain followed by a gasp of surprise from the nearest youth as the teen lost his battle to hold on to his bladder. Their laughter caused my eyes to flash red, but I remembered with regret that I was in the middle of a busy arcade, surrounded by humans and more importantly the new friend that I had made.

"Gotta pick on kids eh?" I yelled, making it sound like my voice was full of false bravado and I swung a loose punch at the lad who had pushed me. I missed his face but connected with his upper arm, but I had pulled my punch so it was probably more like a gnat's breath on his coat, rather than an actual punch.

"Is that all you've got kid?" he sneered at me before lashing out with his fist, punching me in the face. I had turned my head so that I took the force of the hit on my cheek. I cried out in fake pain, my hand going to my face as he followed up with a combination of punches to my stomach and head.

My self-control was being tested to the limit as I fell to the floor, where I felt more than one boot kick my stomach and back and with Jake begging them to leave me alone, I heard the leader snarl.

"Let's get out of here," he hissed. "The slag behind the counter has called the cops." There was a crash as they left, pulling over a stand of sunglasses as they departed and

I pushed myself up onto my hands and knees, playing the part of being hurt.

"Are you okay, Alex?" Jake was kneeling at my side, his hand tentatively touching my back as though he would damage me.

"Just a little bruised, mate," I lied. I knew that I would be showing the effects of the beating and again, I held my control in so that my powers didn't heal me immediately.

"Shit, you look awful," he nearly cried. "Come on, let's get to the bathroom and I'll help clean you up."

"Are you okay, young man?" the woman who had been behind the concessions stand asked, coming over to fuss over me like a mother hen. "They've been causing trouble for the last couple of weeks, so I've called the police this time."

"I'm good, thanks." I needed to get out before the police turned up. Harry would soon find out and then he would try to be all fatherly and limit my solo wanderings. "Come on Jake, looks like you need to clean up as well."

"Huh?" he asked before I pointed to the front of his jeans. There was a dark patch where he had lost control and he flushed bright red.

"Look Jake, don't sweat it," I put an arm around him. "You said you were busting and when that idiot hit you in the stomach, you wouldn't have been able to hold it in."

"JAKE!" I heard a deep voice shout. I looked over, rolling onto the balls of my feet ready to counter another attack.

"It's my Dad," the brown haired teen groaned. "He'll kill me," he whispered before turning and putting on a smile. "Hey Dad, this is Alex."

"What the hell happened?" Mr Norris grabbed his son by the arm. "Why didn't you walk away?"

"You saw?" Jake stopped in his tracks.

"I was over the road in the café."

"Nice of you to help out then," the young teen snapped at his father, a hint of defiance in his voice. "Come on Alex, let's get cleaned up."

"You can do that at home, mister," his father told him. "Then we can talk."

I looked between the two and could see a hint of hostility between them. Not wanting to get in the middle of a family row, but wanting to stand up for my new friend, I started to speak but was cut off by Mr Norris.

"Alex is it?" he asked. "Do you need medical attention or a lift home?"

"Um, no sir. I'll be fine."

"Dad, just let me go and help him clean up and I'll be right out," Jake whined. The pair locked eyes and with a small nod from his father, Jake took my hand and pulled me towards the toilets. We entered the white tiled bathroom, although the whiteness had long since faded into a yellow that I think had more to do with what the room was used for than any other signs of aging.

"Sorry about my Dad," the teen apologised. "He can get a little, ah, over protective at times."

"That's not a bad thing you know," I replied, wincing as I looked in the mirror. I hadn't realised how much damage I had allowed to be inflicted on me. I had two large bruises on the left side of my face, a two inch cut above my right eye which was also showing signs of blackening up already. I knew that I would need to heal it somewhat before getting home, otherwise Harry for one, and Eirwen most definitely would fuss like no tomorrow.

"That looks painful," Jake said softly as he pulled some paper towels from the dispenser and ran the cold water. "I was training to be a first aider at scouts, before we moved here anyway," he shrugged as he saw my questioning stare, before he wiped away the blood from my eye.

"What about your jeans?" I asked. He giggled and before I knew it, I was drenched from the stomach downwards with freezing cold water. "Ah crap, that's cold!" I yelled before acting like the kid that I was supposed to be. I cupped my hands under the tap and threw half a dozen handfuls over the grinning boy.

"Here now, what's going on in here?" an old man asked, walking through the door just as my final salvo hit Jake. "Go on, be out with you. This is a rest room, not a playground."

"Come on, Alex," he laughed. "Let's go and face the music."

We walked back out, water puddling behind us and the frown that spread across Mr Norris's face was worth the fun that we had just had. With another farewell to my new friend and a promise to meet again the following evening, I watched as the pair left. I could sense that the woman behind the counter was fidgeting as though she wanted to come over and mother me some more, but as soon as I heard the heavy footsteps of Blackpool's finest beat patrol, I ducked behind a couple of machines before heading out of the arcade's other exit with my glimmer glyph at full strength.

Michael Andrews

Chapter Five

My moment of peace didn't last long as once again, the voice of the blonde huntress interrupted my thoughts as I sat on a bench overlooking the sea.

"Looks like you may have bitten off a little more than you could chew," Petra chuckled as I turned towards her. She actually winced as she took in the view of my face.

"Not now, please Petra," I sighed. "I'm not in the mood for an argument."

"Why did you let yourself get hit like that?" she asked as she tentatively took a seat next to me on the bench. "I mean, you're quick, one of the quickest vamps I've seen, yet you let yourself get beaten up."

"It's complicated," I replied. "Harry and Eirwen want me to act like a normal kid, to fit in as it were, and if I was to suddenly beat up those four thugs, then Jake would asked questions."

"Jake is it now?" she grinned at me. "You've given up on the whole 'Jake's a werewolf' plot?" I flashed my own grin at her.

"He got taken down far too easily to be a non-human, so yeah, I was wrong," I admitted. "I can make mistakes, you know. I am only fourteen after all."

"Yeah right!" she snorted. "So if it's not Jake and his family, who else could it be?"

I looked at her, hearing the quiver in her voice. She was afraid, which surprised me. After all, she had faced me down the first time that we met with no hint of nervousness in her body. I decided to cut her some slack for now as the possibility of facing a werewolf wasn't something to be taken lightly, especially by a human.

"I dunno," I shrugged. "The old lady behind the counter said that those four bullies had started causing trouble in the last couple of weeks, and to be honest, I can't remember seeing them around here before."

"There are four of them," Petra added. "Their clothes looked ripped and not in the best of states."

"Werewolves do go through a lot of clothes, unless they are prepared for the change," I agreed.

"Maybe we should go and check them out." She stood up and with indecision playing in her green eyes, she reached out her hand. "I still don't like you or anything," she started. "However, Uncle Bill reckons you're okay, and if you can help us get rid of the werewolves, then I'm willing to call a truce."

"I know that you've probably been taught that we are all evil," I stood up, looking at her hand. "But some of us actually do value human lives. I, for one, find the fact that there are werewolves around here very disturbing and I'll do everything I can to get rid of them."

"Even kill them?"

"Especially kill them," I said through gritted teeth. "Eirwen has her reasons for not wanting to kill them, but I have my own for wanting them dead. I'm not going into it," I told her, cutting off her question before she asked.

"Well, I saw them go off down towards the Tower so why don't we have a scout down there."

I took her hand and she pulled me up from the bench. She held her grip for a moment before releasing it and we wandered down the street, side by side. Any onlooker would almost think that we could have been a young couple, but as I tried to put a little distance between us, Petra continued to keep close by my side.

"So have you, like, fought werewolves before?" she asked, the nervousness back in her voice.

"A few times," I replied. "But not in the last couple of hundred years."

"What was it like back then?"

"Back when?" I asked, casting a glance at her.

"When you were with him, ah, with Chlothar," she added.

"I was in Chlothar's House for nearly eight and a half centuries," I frowned at the memories threatening to resurface. "It was a different age to now. The world has changed rapidly since the Industrial Revolution, but even more so in the last fifty years. It was a completely different time when I was born."

"Did you want to be turned, or was it forced upon you?" Petra asked as we stopped to get a drink from a shop. The blonde girl picked up a diet coke while I went for bottled water.

"It's not something that I really like to talk about but it was a mixture, I guess," I admitted. "I wasn't really in a position to say no but I was given the choice."

"So you wanted to become a vampire?"

"I didn't even know they existed until the night that Chlothar turned me," I shuddered at the memory. Even now, more than a thousand years later, I still remember the feel of my sire's fangs as they bit into my neck, his venom pumping through my veins as he saved my life only to be trapped into another form of death.

We walked in silence for a few minutes, both of us lost in thought, both of us scanning the thinning crowds. I could sense tiredness flowing from the young hunter but I didn't want to risk upsetting the truce in our hostilities by suggesting that she went back home.

As we passed the entrance to the Pleasure Beach, my nose picked up a smell that I recognised from before. Holding up a hand to stop Petra, I turned towards the crowds inside and my eyes zoomed in onto the rollercoaster.

"They're on that ride," I announced to her, pointing to the Big One, as it is called.

"You sure?" I cocked my head to the side. "Of course you are, sorry."

"So what do you want to do?" I asked her. "I'll be honest, if they are the wolves, with it being this close to the full moon, I would struggle to take all four on my own."

"You've got me by your side," Petra whispered, her hand going to her side where I could sense the outline of a dirk.

"Why don't we just stroll past them and see if we can sense anything. I can mark them if I'm closer to them and we can come back out tomorrow with your uncle and Eirwen to hunt them down," I suggested.

"Why not take them tonight?"

"Firstly, it's too public. Secondly, if I am going to fight another supernatural creature, I need to feed first. It's been a couple of weeks so I'll need to get my strength up."

I saw her screw her nose up at me and with a shake of my head and a promise that I wasn't going to prey on human flesh, we wandered slowly around the various rides before stopping at the queue for the rollercoaster.

"Come on Gaz, let's go on it again!" the youth who had punched me in the face yelled at the lad whom I had marked as the leader of the four.

"Jesus Sam, how many more times," a second lad moaned. He was looking decidedly green around the gills.

"One more time, come on!" Sam crowed as he pulled the third youth into the queue, while Gaz sauntered behind them, leaving the final member of their gang leaning unsteadily against the rail. I looked at Petra who's eyes were sparkling, but I sensed only at the thought of going on the rollercoaster.

"You go on, and I'll check out Mr Green Gill over there," I offered.

"I don't think we should split up."

"Need me to hold your hand?" I chuckled, getting the look that I deserved in return. I shrugged to myself and got in line with Petra, positioning ourselves half a dozen people behind the three bullies. "I'm too far away from them," I whispered to her, leaning in to make it look like we were exchanging quiet words.

"Well, let's see if we can queue jump," she suggested and with a slight move that I almost missed, she managed to slip inside the couple in front, dragging me along with her. Another couple of minutes in the queue and we were directly behind the four. I turned to try to keep my face covered from them, but the dark haired Sam appeared to be too observant.

"Oh hello, it looks like you want another round with us, eh kid?" he sneered.

"Um, no mate," I stammered out, putting the sound of fear in my voice.

"Where's your pissy mate gone?" the other laughed.

"He's gone home," I replied. "Look, I don't want no trouble, just to ride this beast with my friend."

"Your girlfriend, you mean?" Sam pushed me. "You can do a lot better than this pipsqueak, darling," he leered at Petra.

"He can't fight for shit," the third added, while I noticed the leader, Gaz, standing back, taking it all in. "You should go out with a real man."

"Well boys, when you find a real man, let me know where he is," Petra fired back. "In the meantime, I'll stick with this one." Turning to me, she caught me by surprise by grabbing me and pulling me towards her before planting her lips on mine. My instant reactionary thought was to pull away, but realising that would give away that we weren't there for the rollercoaster, I made a show of kissing Petra back.

"Frigging hell, he's punched well above his weight," Sam complained as he turned back to face forwards, his interest in us waning.

The queue moved forwards with Petra now holding my hand, a mysterious smile on her face. Conflicting emotions ran through my body and mind. Of course, she had only kissed me to keep our disguise and let's face it, she's a hunter. I shook the thoughts of inappropriate romance out of my head and concentrated on trying to feel out any paranormal senses from the three guys in front of us.

As the rollercoaster came to a halt and the occupants staggered off, it was our turn to get in. I looked at Petra with an unasked question in my expression and the silent response was given as she climbed into the empty carriage. I took a seat next to her with the couple that we had slipped in front of taking the two seats behind us. We were positioned in the carriage behind the three youths and I tried to get my empathic powers to feel them out but before I had a chance to fully concentrate, the ride started up and I spent the next few minutes grimly hanging on to the safety bar.

As it pulled to a stop, Petra grinned as she watched me get of the ride on shaky legs.

"I thought that you would enjoy that!" she chuckled.
"I prefer being in charge of my own flight, not at the mercy of a metal contraption that could derail at any time," I stammered. My stomach was doing a fine impression of a back flip as I took deep breaths to steady my nerves.

"I wouldn't have thought that you were scared of a little ride," Petra nudged me in the direction of the four lads who were arguing about what they were going to do next.

"Remind me when this is all over and I'll take you flying," I shot a grin at her. "We won't need a ride or a plane."

"So, did you get anything from them?" We were walking past them and as I let my mind open, I was frustrated that I couldn't sense anything from them. I shook my head before we walked back onto the sea front.

"Come on, let's get back home," I said, annoyed that the mystery was still there. Deciding to get my own back for the ride, I guided the blonde into a side street. Looking around to make sure that we were unseen, I took hold of her waist.

"Hey now, less of that!" she gasped at me.

"Trust me," I smiled and jumped into the air. I nearly had to stop on two or three occasions as her high pitched scream echoed into my left ear as Petra clung on to me for dear life, before I landed softly in the communal gardens outside the homes of Harry and Bill. I saw the pair come rushing out of Harry's patio door, Bill immediately going up to his niece to check that she was unharmed.

"What happened to you?" Harry asked, lifting my face to the light. I'd forgotten about my bruises and cuts and shrugged.

"Just getting my undercover identity in place. Some lads wanted to cause trouble with Jake and me so I couldn't beat them up."

"Well, let's get you fixed up," he tried to lead me inside, but Petra grabbed my arm.

"Don't ever do that again!" she started, before a smile broke across her face. "At least without warning me first. That was amazing! Much better than the Big One."

"I'll take you to the top of the Tower next time," I replied, before adding under my breath, "and maybe I'll leave you up there if you scream in my ear again!"

Harry cocked his head as he looked between the two of us before flashing a look at Bill. They said their goodnights before we went our separate ways into the houses. Harry led me to the kitchen where he pulled out a bag of ice to put on my eye.

"You know that this is a waste of time, don't you?" I laughed.

"Well, it makes me feel better," he shrugged. "So you didn't find anything out?"

"I'm fairly sure that it isn't the Norris's, or at least it isn't Jake. But there were these four lads who certainly looked the part, but I couldn't get a feel from them."

"That could mean something? That you couldn't, I mean. Can they mask their presence like you can?"

"I don't want to believe that they can," I frowned. "A werewolf with abilities is not what we want to evolve."

"DCI Bach, Eirwen and Y'cart were round earlier. She's quite nice, really, isn't she?"

"Who? The DCI?"

"No. Y'cart. I can see why the recent movies have portrayed witches as good looking."

I looked at Harry for a moment and I was suddenly hit by a powerful surge of affection flowing from him.

"Um, Harry. She's a witch and long lived, you know. She's at least six hundred years old."

"Yeah, I know," he replied with a confused look on his face.

"She sees the world differently to you. Her desires aren't the same as a normal woman, and I would get in so much trouble if she heard me say that."

"I'll make sure not to tell her," Harry smiled.

"So what were they here for?"

"Who?"

"The women?" I sighed as I felt his mind wandering off with thoughts of the dark haired witch .

"Oh. Well, Eirwen thinks that Y'cart can help find out who the lycans are but we'll need something from them."

"Like what?"

"A piece of clothing, some hair, anything that has been in contact with them."

"But how can we get that if we don't know who they are in the first place?" I sighed in frustration.

"Sorry, I'm not explaining it well I guess. Y'cart has a spell that will show if a person actually is the werewolf, so if you think you know, we can test them out and prove it either way."

"Well, it's a start," I yawned. "I'll go back out tomorrow and hunt down those four guys."

"You could take Petra with you," Harry suggested, a sly smile on his face.

"Why?"

"Well, you seem to be getting along better," he replied. "I almost thought that you looked like, you know, friends."

"Urgh! Don't! She even kissed me earlier, but just as a disguise."

"Sure it was," Harry punched my arm. "It's never too early to go get the girl."

"Oh puh-lease," I huffed, getting up from the table. "That is never going to happen. I need to sleep, and can you tell the DCI that I'll need to feed in the next forty eight hours, especially if we're going up against lycans."

I saw him nod before I turned and left the kitchen, heading upstairs. I resisted the temptation to watch the CCTV clip once again, something that had become a habit in the last couple of weeks. Instead, I jumped into bed, closing the drapes behind me.

Michael Andrews

Chapter Six

I crept through the forest on silent feet, well, as silent as I could make them. The sun's rays were still shining through the canopy, casting beams of yellow light onto the forest greenery. I paused for a moment as a young deer stopped twenty yards in front of me, feeding on the grassy floor.

A snap of a twig under my foot caused the chocolate coloured foal to look up and straight at me, it's dark black eyes narrowing as it contemplated if I was a threat. I held my breath, hoping that the beautiful creature would continue to remain motionless but in an instant, it turned and leapt away, bounding through the undergrowth and to safety.

Sighing to myself, I walked out into the sun, stretching my arms to catch the heat of the late autumn sun before the chill of winter once again gripped our small village. Voices echoed through the woods and I paused, my hand going to my hunting knife that my mother and stepfather had given to me on my fourteenth birthday. It was my coming of age present, marking me as a man, ready to take my place and responsibilities in the village.

"Where have you got to, you damn sheep!" I hissed to myself, worried that the stray animal would wander into the path of strangers, of the bandits who had been raiding the nearby villages. "Father will have my guts for his garter if I don't bring you back."

"Now that's something I'd like to see," a girlish voice giggled, causing me to spin on the spot, my knife held out on front of me as the fighting men of the village had taught me.

"Oh, I'm sorry," I dropped my arm as I saw the fearful expression on the blonde girl stood twenty yards away from me. "I thought that you were a robber or something."

"Me? A robber?" the girl giggled again, a smile on her face that reminded me of the rising sun. "Don't be silly."

"What are you doing here?" I asked, looking around. "It's dangerous to be out in the woods on your own."

"Oh piffle!" she replied. "My father's guards say that all the time, but nothing has ever happened yet."

"Your father?"

Any further conversation was cut off as three armed soldiers burst into the small clearing, their swords drawn. I gulped and took a step backwards, hiding my knife behind me so that they didn't get the wrong idea. They wore the uniform of the Earl, a man not to be trifled with.

"There you are m'Lady," one of the guards huffed. "You shouldn't slip away like that."

"Who are you, boy?" a second asked as they noticed me.

"Um, I'm Alexander," I stammered as the two approached me. "I'm just looking for my sheep."

"A sheepherder eh?" the taller of the two sneered. "Well, go find your sheep and leave our Lady Catherine alone."

"Lady Catherine?" I gasped, as I looked at the girl. I knew of her, of course, but had only ever seen her from afar. Up close, she was much more beautiful than I ever imagined.

"Oh bother!" she sighed. "There goes my chance of finding out if you liked me for me."

"My Lady, we need to return to the castle," the lead soldier instructed.

"Very well," Lady Catherine replied. She turned to me and flashed me a smile. "Maybe we'll meet again, Alexander."

"I hope so, my Lady," I tried to bow as I had seen others do.

"I wouldn't, lad," the last soldier turned to me as his companions left. "Take it from me lad, her father is a right bastard who dotes on his only daughter. She's going to marry some duke's son, or even a prince, so if he hears that you've even spoken to her, well, let's just say that you'd be best moving."

"What would he do?" I gulped.

"You'd probably meet the wrong end of a blade and be left in a ditch somewhere," he reached out to ruffle my hair. "Forget about her and go bed a nice buxom lass from the village eh?"

"I'm thirteen," I blushed. "I'm too young for all of that."

"There's younger fathers than you around here lad," he told me. "Just be careful and stay away from the Lady Catherine for your own sake."

I watched as he turned and followed the rest of his group out of the small clearing, a frown on my face at the warning. Surely the Earl wouldn't kill me just for talking to his daughter, would he? I looked back at the group and was surprised to see the blonde girl turn back at the last minute. She gave me a smile that sent goosebumps all over my body and I raised my hand in farewell to her.

I awoke with a start. It had been a couple of hundred years since I had dreamed about Catherine, my first love. Even at that early age, I knew that I had fallen for my Earl's daughter. It was a completely different time in those days, and the guard was quite right. You were considered a man once you could pick up a sword and fight, bring home food for your family and also have certain body parts in full working order.

I shook my head to clear it. I didn't need any reminders about what I had lost weighing me down. My hand automatically went to my stomach, feeling for the non-existent scar that had long since vanished after I had been turned by Chlothar. I had more important matters to concern myself with than thoughts of long lost loves. Where had that even come from anyway?

I got up and dressed quickly, grabbing my usual attire of black before heading downstairs. Surprisingly the kitchen was empty for a change. In fact, the whole house was empty. I found a note stuck to the fridge from Harry telling me that he'd had to leave early for a meeting at the station and, without a better plan, I decided to pay Y'cart a visit.

Landing on soft feet after the brief flight over the town, I looked at the house of the witch and was, in a way, a little disappointed. Instead of the cottages of old, with a smoking chimney and broomsticks outside, Y'cart was living in what looked to be a nice three bedroom detached house. No thatched roof, just a normal tiled one and double glazed windows to keep out the cold, winter wind that blew in over the Irish Sea.

"I was wondering when you'd come around," the deep, rich voice of Eirwen's favourite witch greeted me as she opened the door.

"I can't believe that you've got spells set up to track me," I frowned. "If Eirwen says that you're okay, then you have nothing to fear from me. Besides, you've saved my life twice so I am in debt to you."

"Don't have such a high opinion of yourself, Alexander," Y'cart smiled at me. "I happened to be looking out of the window when I saw you land."

"Oh. That's alright then." She ushered me inside and again, I was a little disappointed to see that her house looked normal in every way. She caught me looking around.

"I've left the cauldron in the garage," she chuckled before walking through into the kitchen.

"Now this is more like it," I grinned as I saw bottle after bottle of various concoctions on the shelves. I ran my finger along the lowest shelf, just at my eye level. "Eh? Strawberry, blackcurrant, marmalade?"

"What were you expecting? Eye of newt and toe of frog jam?"

"Jam?"

"I have a small but profitable online business selling jam," Y'cart told me. "I have to earn money somehow and the days of love potions are long since forgotten."

"Did they really work or was it just a scam for the gullible?" I asked, curious to figure out one of life's great mysteries.

"Oh yes, some of the potions really did work, but it was a fake love, a chemically induced one," she frowned. "Sometimes, people only needed a placebo to give them the confidence to express their true feelings."

"But you could change people's emotions with a potion?" The hair on the back of my neck bristled as she nodded.

"Alcohol and many other drugs changes people's emotions all of the time. That's all that a potion really is, a mixture of different drugs."

I took the offered bottle of water from her, carefully checking it to make sure it was sealed, which brought a smile back to her face. I knew that she knew some of my history and as I gulped down a couple of mouthfuls, she turned to me once more.

"So what brings you willingly into my house, Alexander?"

"Harry said that you'd come up with a way of identifying the lycans. I was going to go hunting and wanted to know what you needed."

"The person ideally," she chuckled. "Alive of course, but really, any part of their body will suffice."

"What? Like a limb?" I gasped.

"Well, you do still have that big old sword of yours. How you managed to get Auron to part with it, I'd love to find out one of these days."

"That's between him and me," I muttered, thinking back to my darker past. "You seriously want me to go around chopping bits of our suspects?"

"Of course not," Y'cart snapped at me. "I just need something that has got their DNA on it."

"Like a piece of hair or something?"

"Or something that they have drank from, like that bottle of water you're drinking. I can take a swab of saliva from it and work with that."

"How will you know?"

"There's a spell I've been working on that should indicate if a person isn't entirely human."

"Should indicate?" I pressed. "We have to be one hundred percent sure. I'm not going to go around killing innocents."

"Don't worry about it. Eirwen has every confidence that it will work fine."

I muttered a curse under my breath. As lovely and beautiful as my pretend mother was, she was still the vicious killer that Chlothar had trained her to be. She was more ruthless than I was, probably why I had been chosen for the role of bodyguard to my sire while Eirwen was frequently deployed as his assassin. Nodding a farewell to the witch, I leapt into the air, making sure that my glimmer glyph was in place and cruised over towards the Pleasure Beach.

Landing in a back street, I shed the glyph and walked around to the main promenade. My nose picked up the various smells and delights that come with living in Blackpool. The smell of the sea breeze covered up some of the more unpleasant smells, those of the drunken yobs staggering out of the nearest pubs while they looked for either their next drink, their next fight or simply their next spot to vomit into.

However, mixed in with all of that was the definite scent of lupine sweat. I had to fight to remain calm, my vampire instincts screaming at my body to come to the fore in order to protect myself from any threat. I cursed, reminding myself that I still needed to feed to be at full strength for any confrontation with a werewolf and as I turned into the arcade, my eyes fixed onto the four youths from the previous evening.

I felt my fangs begin to break the flesh of my gums as I stood, watching them playing on the zombie game that Jake and I had been playing. I bided my time, putting some money into one of the fruit machines where I could keep them in view.

"ALEX!" an enthusiastic voice from behind made me jump, dropping three pound coins onto the floor. I bent down to pick them up and found myself staring into two pools of chocolate brown. My throat constricted and I had to force myself to break the gaze. Looking to the side, I saw a smiling Jake.

"You remember my sister?" he asked, indicating the girl in front of me.

"Um, yeah. Sarah isn't it?" I stammered as my gaze returned to her eyes.

"Sarah-Louise actually," she sighed. "Our parents couldn't decide on which of our Grandmas to name me after so I got both."

"Thank god they didn't have that argument about me," Jake sniggered. "Can you imagine being called Alfred-Wilhelm!"

"Wilhelm?" I asked. "Bit of a weird name for a Londoner."

"Our Mum's side is from Germany originally so they like to keep the old names going," the lad replied.

"Saxony actually," his sister piped up. "I was hoping to find out that we were related to the royal family, but we're not."

"Eh? Why would you be?"

"Before they changed their name to Windsor, they were called the Saxe-Cobergs," she shrugged. "I could just see me as a princess."

"Yeah, like the one out of Shrek when she's an ogre!" Jake giggled, earning a push from the slightly taller girl.

"So what are you guys doing out?" I asked, trying to balance being friendly with them and wanting to get away so that I could concentrate on the youths.

"Our parents are having a beer and I said that I'd show her the arcade," Jake replied. "I was gonna show her the zombie game but they're there." He nodded over in the direction of the lads.

"Are they the ones who hit you?" Sarah-Louise asked menacingly. I could see her hands balling into fists. She looked at my face, as if noticing the bruises for the first time. She reached out a hand and held my head to the side.

"They're the ones, but let's just leave it," I told her. "We don't need any more trouble."

"If they hit you, and my brother, then I want to know why," she hissed. I didn't need any of my empathic powers to sense the hostility and venom that was pouring from the dark haired girl. The hairs on my arms stood up as I felt a surge of power kick through the arcade, something that it seemed most people felt as they paused for a moment before continuing to push coins into slot machines. The lad I knew as Gaz turned for a brief moment, his eyes searching the scene before they flicked over to where we were standing. His eyes met mine for a second and widen in recognition before he took in the other two. He shrugged to himself and turned back to watch two of the others on the machine continue to splat their enemies.

"Look, they're obviously tough nuts and who knows if they've got blades or something," I countered, trying to keep the girl away from the pack of lads.

"I don't care about blades, I can handle that," the girl announced bravely.

"Yeah, she does Jugunji," Jake nodded.

"Ju-jitsu, dummy," Sarah-Louise poked him. I was thinking that she would be a great match for Petra.

"Well, martial arts or not, it's best to leave them alone," I suggested, turning to walk away from the group to try to get Jake and his sister to follow. The last thing that I wanted to do was put them in danger. I got a harrumph from Sarah-Louise, but was pleased to see them follow me out of the arcade and onto the pier.

Michael Andrews

Chapter Seven

After making small talk with them for around thirty minutes, I managed to excuse myself and returned to the arcade. Of course, the lads had moved on. Nothing in my life was ever that easy, but as I wandered from arcade to arcade, shop to shop, I caught a glimpse of them sitting on a bench overlooking the sea, drinking from a pack of lager.

I stood watching them, trying to figure out a way of bumping into them to rip a piece of their clothing without being too obvious, but nothing came to mind. I sighed in frustration as the one called Sam missed his throw into the rubbish bin, his scrunched up empty can rattling around the rim before bouncing noisily onto the floor.

"You're such a crap shot!" laughed the lad who was going to be sick after the ride yesterday.

"Sod off Billy!" Sam cursed back, giving him the finger.

"Haven't seen you make one yet," Gaz offered in a conciliatory tone, heading off what looked like a situation that would easily spill into a fight. Both lads settled back down, to me a sure sign that Gaz was the Alpha of the pack.

A gust of wind blew from the sea and I felt the hair on my neck stand up again as the smell of wolf filled my nostrils. I was more convinced than ever that I had found the werewolves. Remembering that Y'cart had told me that she could test them from something that they had drunk out of, I waited for them to pick up the remaining bag of full cans and saunter off down the promenade before I scooted over and grabbed all the discarded cans. Putting them into an empty carrier bag that I had caught drifting along in the wind, I saw an elderly couple nod appreciatively in my direction, obviously thinking that I was cleaning up. Nodding to them to allow them their fantasy, I turned and left the sea front, walking down a side street.

"Never figured that vamps would be the 'save the Earth' types," the familiar voice of Petra sniggered.

"We've done more for this planet than humans ever will," I snapped back. Talk about having a bad day get worse.

"Oh yeah, you really do go out of the way to clean up the environment," she replied, the sneer back in her voice. It looked like any truce that we had come to the previous evening was over.

"Well, we try to cut down the number of humans who pollute the planet, but for some reason the rodents keep multiplying." I felt her emotions bristle before a strong hand gripped my shoulder firmly.

"Do you two have to argue every time that you see each other?" Bill sighed as he stepped from the shadows.

"She started it," I began to say before realising that I would sound like a whiney teenage boy, something that I certainly was not. "What are you doing here?"

"Following up on your lead about the lads being the pack," the old hunter explained. "Though it is interesting why you're cleaning up their beer cans."

"Community spirit?" I smiled, but knew that I wouldn't get away with the reply. "The witch says that she has figured out a way of identifying the lycans from their DNA, so these cans will have some on them. I was going to take them to her to check out if these lads are definitely the scum we're looking for before I kill them."

"You're sure that they can't be reasoned with?" Petra asked. "I mean, if they agree not to kill anything, can't we like, just leave each other alone?"

"Some hunter," I muttered, getting poked in the rib by the old man to keep my thoughts to myself. "Lycans don't play nice," I explained. "They mark their ranges. Anything that comes into it that is a potential danger or power is attacked."

"So you're at risk then," Bill queried, picking up on a point that both Y'cart and Harry had ignored.

"So is Eirwen," I nodded before looking at the pair and in a quiet voice added, "And so are you two."

"US?" Petra gasped.

"You're both trained hunters and while not falling under the supernaturally gifted, you're still forces to be reckoned with and, to a lycan, you're also a potential predator. Once they discover your existence, they will hunt you down and kill you."

"Then we need to find out if these boys are definitely the wolves and do something about them," Bill stated. "Alex, you take those cans to Y'cart while Petra and I trail these lads. They have to live somewhere, so knowing where it is will cut down the time it takes to track them later."

I had already launched myself into the air and was catching a current before I realised that I had followed a human's orders without any question. I shook my head, muttering about the situation forcing my continued cooperation with hunters before landing back at Y'cart's house.

She must have been watching out of the window again as, when I approached the door, the witch had already opened it, beckoning me inside. Handing her the bag, I followed her into the kitchen.

"Ah, there you are, Alex," Harry smiled at me as he drank from a mug. My nose picked up the strong smell of filter coffee and my eyes lit up as I saw a nearly full jug on the side.

"Did you have any trouble?" Eirwen asked as she eased to one side, moving out of my path as I headed towards Harry and my cup of black delight.

"Ah, that's better," I smiled, finally getting something good out of the day. "I'd have preferred to have trailed them for a while but, first, I got cornered by Jake and his sister, then Bill and Petra bumped into me."

"Bill? What's he doing?" Harry asked about his neighbour.

"They're off following the lads to see if they can find their lair," I said between long sips. I could feel the warmth of the dark liquid inside me.

"Will they be okay?" he asked. "I mean, if they are the werewolves, will the two of them be able to defend themselves?"

"Until they shift form, the lads are simply humans, albeit it gaining strength as the full moon approaches, but nothing that a hunter can't cope with," Eirwen explained. "However, once they transform, humans are no match strengthwise. The only reason that hunters and some other humans survive is intelligence and instinct."

"Do wolves take their human intelligence over into their animal form?" Vanessa asked, walking into the kitchen, her nephew Jason trailing in behind her. The little imp was struggling with a heavy bag which I scooted over and relieved him of.

"Thanks Alex," he smiled at me. "That was hurting my shoulder."

Y'cart frowned at the DCI as she beckoned the ten year old to her. He bounced over to the witch, popping in the offered sweet before standing in front of her as she massaged his shoulder. I gave her a sideways glance which she laughed at.

"Not all witches try to trap the likes of Hansel and Gretel," she chuckled. "However, they were both little brats that deserved to be killed. That's why they were lured into the woods in the first place."

"They were real?" Vanessa gasped. "I just thought that they were a tale."

"Oh no, they were real enough. They were little monsters who enjoyed torturing animals, something that offends witches as we are the ones who are most in tune with nature," Y'cart replied.

"You'll find that most of the so called fairy tales are based on reality," Eirwen explained. "The Comitia wrote them to warn the humans about the paranormal. It was the first exercise in mass propaganda in our battle."

"But I thought that the Grimm Brothers wrote them," the DCI argued.

"They did," I told her. "We aren't the only ones who have had friends in powerful positions. The Grimm Brothers disliked our kind but it didn't stop them earning a great deal of money from us."

"Anyway, you two need to feed before this blood goes off," Vanessa pointed to the bag that I'd placed on the worktop. "I organised an impromptu blood drive at the Town Hall and we've brought sixteen pints. I thought that should be enough for the two of you."

"It's O Neg!" Jason jumped up, getting our attention. "I made sure that Auntie Ness got you O Neg."

"Well done, buddy," I ruffled his hair, before catching myself doing it. God! I'm turning into Harry! I shot him a look and he must have been reading my mind as he was covering up a snigger. I frowned at myself but Jason was lapping up the attention. I knew that he adored anything vampirey so I reached into an inside pocket on my black hoodie and pulled out a small blade. I held my hand out to him.

"What's that?" he asked, his eyes widening as he saw the silver weapon.

"This, Jason, was given to me by my former Captain, the one who trained me how to fight," I explained. I fingered the ebony handle. It was only one of three things that I had kept following Eirwen's and my escape from the House of Chlothar. I reversed my grip, handing it to the young boy.

"Wow! Look at this knife!" Jason gushed as he held it up to light, which reflected off its surface.

"Are you sure that's safe?" Vanessa asked, a worried expression on her face.

"Jason is bonded and therefore is a potential danger to the lycans. I want him to be able to defend himself at least," I replied before turning back to the boy. "The blade is made from silver so it will hurt a werewolf. If one comes anywhere near you, just stab at it, or slice it and it should back off and look for an easier prey."

"Way coooool!" the ten year old bounced on the spot, just as Y'cart took the blade from him before he poked himself with it and slipped it into a sheath. She handed it back to him, the lad's momentary frown being replaced by his usual smile.

"Let's feed," Eirwen suggested and for the next half an hour, the two of us drained the bags of blood, trying to ignore the looks from the Harry and Jason who were not yet used to watching blood being drunk.

While we were ignoring the rest, Y'cart had busied herself with the empty beer cans, placing them into a selection of saucepans that were heating on her gas fired stove. I turned up my nose and walked outside, Harry following me.

"What's up?" he asked as I took in a deep breath of crisp November air.

"Why witches brews have to smell so god-damned awful is beyond me," I gagged.

"I couldn't really smell anything," he replied, coming to the defence of Y'cart. I could sense that loving feeling emanating from him again, which I chose to ignore.

"I've got better senses remember," I let him off. "I forgot how fresh it can be up here."

"You have been in England before then?" Harry queried.

"Yeah, I was born not too far from here actually," I smiled in memory. "My village was a small one, just on the outskirts of the Earl's city."

"Which one? I mean, is it a city that's still here?"

"Nah, it was destroyed centuries ago," I sighed. "My former master wanted to teach me a lesson."

"He destroyed a city to teach you a lesson? What lesson?" he gasped.

"Power and revenge. It was too late to get revenge on the Earl of my time but by wiping out his descendants, it sent a message to the rest of the ruling Lords about what happens if you cross a vampire."

"Did you, you know, take part?" I could sense the unease flowing from him as I nodded.

"Look Harry, I know that you look at me and see a fourteen year old boy. In some ways, I am still a fourteen year old. There are parts of me that will never grow up, never change from the mindset of being fourteen, but you have to remember that I am a thousand years old and a vampire to boot."

"So you helped kill those people?"

I nodded, walking away from him to stare at the near full moon. I heard his footsteps on the gravel driveway approach me from behind.

"Look Alex, I know that sometimes I look at you and fall into the trap thinking that you are just a normal kid, but I'm trying my best to get my head around it." He put his hand on my shoulder. "I also know that while you have done things in the past, you aren't that type of person, um, that type of vampire anymore."

"You're wrong," I whispered.

"What do you mean?"

"I mean that I will do anything and everything in my power to stop these werewolves from striking again and if it means sacrificing humans, then I will."

"Well, we better make sure it doesn't come to that," he clapped my back, turning me back towards him. I let a weak smile break across my face before we both turned at the sound of the front door opening.

"Y'cart's potions have finished," Vanessa announced, turning back inside.

We followed her in and walked back into the kitchen. The mood was grim and my hackles went into vamp mode before I took some deep breaths. The odour of lycan filled the room.

"It's them!" I hissed and bolted for the door. I threw myself into the air, catching the nearest air current with the sound of Eirwen and Y'cart's shouts of warning ringing in my ears. There was no way that I was going to put them in harm's way if I could help it. I made a brief stop at home to pick up my sword, strapping it over my back before flying back out over the town. I opened my mind, casting my thoughts over the ground below as I circled, searching for the wolf pack, ready to wipe them out before they could kill again.

I knew that I would have no luck in locating Bill. He was far too experienced for me to be able to find him easily, so instead I concentrated on the easier target. Picking up the now familiar feel of Petra's mind, I sniffed the air and recognised her scent. My eyes honed in on a shabby looking terraced house on one of the rougher estates of Blackpool and after making sure that my glimmer glyph was in place, I landed on silent feet.

Chapter Eight

I drew my sword from the sheath on my back, holding the hilt in my right hand. I decided not to extend the blade just yet as, with it being a magically enhanced sword, it would fight against my own spell. I crept along the darkened street, hugging the shadows which were numerous thanks to every other street lamp being smashed or torn down. I let my mind open to the surroundings, reaching out to try to feel every living creature that moved around me. It was easy enough to ignore the multitude of rats that infested the gardens, feeding upon the overflowing rubbish bins that the council had failed to collect on their latest rounds.

I felt the various humans, believing they were safe in their houses, not knowing the danger that lurked on their estate, or indeed in the world in general. A werewolf could easily smash through a door to hunt down its prey. I continued along the street until I found the essence of minds that I was searching for. Mind you, it would have been easy enough without my powers as the four lads were sitting outside, music blaring from a stereo and a fresh pile of empty cans by the side of the probably stolen pub garden table that they were seated around.

This was it. The simple solution to the immediate problem. I could hit them now before the lunar change came and ensure that they killed no other innocents. With my sword's command word on my lips, I edged closer to the garden, noting that there were several twitching curtains as upset neighbours were being kept awake by the loud music from the youths. Obviously they must be known to the neighbourhood as I noted that, while I felt a great deal of resentment and anger from the surrounding houses, not a single person had ventured out to put a stop to the noise.

It did, however, give me a problem. With the curtain twitchers as an audience, I would have to adapt my plan of attack. I pulled up my hoodie, covering my blonde hair and sat on my haunches for a few moments, watching and waiting for inspiration. The thought flashed across my mind that I could go wolf on the wolves; the ultimate irony would also give me a cover story but, conversely, the news about a large wolf being seen in the town would cause undue attention being brought to Blackpool.

In the end, I settled for a plan that had worked well for me in the past, that of the annoying teenager. I re-sheathed my sword, picked up a couple of medium sizes stones and crept close the garden fence.

"Take that you gits!" I shouted as I stood and threw the rocks. My aim, of course, was true. I knocked the stereo from the table; the smashing sound as it hit the floor I was sure would be the best sound in the world to all the neighbours. My next two throws caught Sam square on the jaw, dropping him face down on the floor while Gaz fended off the stone aimed at him.

"You little bastard!" he cursed at me, jumping up. "What are you doing?"

"Payback's a bitch!" I crowed, my final stone knocking the beer from Billy's hand with a satisfying crunch as he howled at his now broken fingers.

"It's that little runt from the arcade," the last remaining unknown lad shouted. "Let's grab him."

"You've gotta catch me first," I giggled like the kid I was supposed to be and gave them the one fingered salute before turning and running off down the street. I could hear all four giving chase, albeit Sam slowly bringing up the rear and as I darted around the various side streets and alleys of the estate, I had to slow several times to allow them to remain within a reasonable distance of me.

"Bloody hell, the kid can run," I heard Billy huff.

"He won't be running after we got hold of him," I heard Gaz's voice echo sinisterly around the corner. I had paused, letting them catch up so that they were only a few yards away from me. I had spotted a dark cul-de-sac where two buildings backed on to each other and, as the lads turned the corner, I pretended to be out of breath, leaning against the wall.

"Oh crap!" I yelled, pretending that I'd just seen them.

"That's right, kid. You ain't getting away from us, so just make it easy and come here!" the still unnamed lad snarled.

"Sod that!" I huffed and turned to run, deliberately aiming for the darkened alley before stopping half way down it.

"There's no getting out of there, kid!" Sam cackled as the four slowed to a walking pace, spreading out to cover the width of the alley. I turned back to look at them, forcing a look of panic and fear onto my face. Hey, when you studied with some of the best Shakespearean actors of their time, you pick up a few tricks. I received some fair praise for my role of Prince Edward in Richard III when it first debuted in Paris, but that was a long time ago.

"Um, look," I stammered out. "I'm really sorry 'bout breaking your stereo, but I just wanted to hit you after you beat me up."

"You picked on the wrong guys to get revenge, brat," the one lad hissed but as he took a step forward, Gaz put out a hand, stopping him moving towards me.

"Hold on Jim. You've got balls, kid," the leader of the four said. "I like that."

"What? He broke my bloody fingers, Gaz!" Billy moaned, holding up his hand which showed two of his digits at a definitely different angle to the rest.

"You should learn how to catch then," I chuckled. "Do you want to try it again?" I bent down and picked up a stone that I had scuffed with my trainer as I'd turned.

"Sod off, kid! Put the stone down or I'll smash your face in," Billy snapped back.

"You will need to pay for smashing our stereo," Gaz said, stepping towards me. "You look like you're from a well off family so how much money have you got on you?"

"What? I ain't paying for that piece of crap," I hissed, taking a step backwards. I had calculated that I could back myself into a corner, which would only further increase the likelihood of the lads attacking me. I could sense that the three were desperate for a little fighting action but Gaz was an enigma. I couldn't get a clear read of him, which only further confirmed that he was the Alpha.

"Unless you cough up, kid, we're gonna hurt ya."

"Well, I ain't got no money on me. Oh wait," I paused and pulled out a handful of notes. I held them up for the lads to see.

"Bloody hell, the kid's loaded. There must be at least two hundred there."

"Let's get it, kick the shit out of him and go home," Billy suggested, hope evident in his voice.

"Sorry guys but I was always told not to give money to down and outs," I laughed and slowly ripped up the notes. Disbelief flowed from them before their faces screwed up into grimaces of anger.

"You're so dead now, kid. Let's get him!"

The four charged me at once. With it being only one night away from the full moon, I was disappointed about how easily I avoided their punches. It was almost like they weren't actually trying to hurt me as I deflected hit after hit, not one of them landing a blow on me.

"I guess that the rumours about you guys are all a load of bull," I sighed as I ducked under a poor attempt of a roundhouse kick from Sam.

"What rumours?" Billy paused in his attack. I took the opening and grabbed his broken hand, pulling him towards me easily and squeezed, crushing the bones of his unbroken fingers in my grip. I silenced his pitiful yelps of pain as I span him around and pushed him at the wall, his head bouncing off the brickwork to leave him unconscious on the rubbish strewn floor.

"Shit, kid! You shouldn't have done that," Jim swore and the three rushed me all from different angles.

As my vamp senses kicked in, I didn't even feel the punches that rained in on my arms and back in the thirty seconds that it took me to render the three unconscious. I paused, wiping the small trickle of sweat that had built up on my brow before looking down at the four fallen werewolves. I reached for my sword, happy in the knowledge that the magic entrenched in the blade would finish off any paranormal creature.

"Alex!" Bill's voice hissed from behind me. I span, my nails extended at the unexpected interruption.

"Bill!" I snarled at him. "You should know better than to creep up on me. What are you doing here?"

"Petra and I were just about to leave for home when you turned up," he started.

"And we aren't letting you kill these lads so move away from them," Petra snarled at me. She had her crossbow out and even with my supernatural speed, I still took in a gulp of air as I saw it pointed directly at my heart.

"But these are the lycans," I hissed. "I knew that I shouldn't have trusted a human to do the job."

"They're not," Bill interrupted me as I was about to embark on a rant about the duplicity of the pair.

"What do you mean? Y'cart's spell identified them," I explained. "I could smell the stench of lycan throughout her house so move aside and let me finish what we came here to do." I paused. "Or do you want more human deaths on your hands?"

"Harry has been trying to reach you since you left the house," the old hunter said, a calming tone to his voice. "Y'cart's potion cleared them of all suspicion, and when the DCI asked how she knew, the witch put in a hair of a werewolf. That was what you smelled."

"That's bullshit," I spat. "Why would Y'cart carry around a hair of a werewolf?"

"Because it is an ingredient in a cure spell," I heard the soft voice of Eirwen behind me. I turned and watched her land a few yards down the alleyway. "You really need to keep your phone turned on, son."

I gritted my teeth and reached into the inner pocket of my hoodie and fished out my phone. It was powered off. I hit the power button and saw it flicker into life, only to shut down once more.

"The battery's dead," I sighed. "I guess I must have forgotten to charge it when I went to bed this morning."

"Well, it's a good job that Bill and Petra were still here then," my mother breathed a sigh of relief. "Y'cart was showing us what the brew should have smelled like if these were the lycans when you walked in. She didn't think to call you as you can already recognise the smell of a fully converted lycan, thanks to Paulinos."

"Well, they deserved a good kicking anyway," I shrugged and turned to leave, before turning back to Bill. "What made you so sure that they weren't the lycans. I mean, I can't believe that you would have just accepted the word of a witch." I felt Eirwen bristle and reminded myself that I had to watch what I called Y'cart while she was around.

"It was the oldest form of confirmation in the book," Bill chuckled. "They had a pet cat."

Michael Andrews

80

Chapter Nine

"A cat!" I hissed. "Let me guess, it was black!"

"Actually it was tabby," Petra replied, lowering her crossbow, much to my relief. "Uncle Bill said that no small cat would live in the same house as a werewolf, even in human form."

"Bill is correct in that," Eirwen added. "Sorry Alexander, but these boys are not the werewolves. The pack is somewhere else."

"We're running out of time," I said, frustration in my voice. "It's a full moon tomorrow which means that they can kill anytime for the next four days."

"The moon is full for four days?" Petra queried. "I thought it was only like, a day or something."

"Lady Luna is considered to be in her glory when she reaches ninety five percent luminosity," Eirwen explained. "That means that she is at her full energy for three to four nights, depending on the time of the year."

"Well, just because that's true, doesn't mean that they will be out each night," Petra paused. "Does it?"

"Lycans aren't shape shifters, Petra," Bill said quietly. "They cannot control when they turn. The lunar energy is what turns them so yes, they will be out each and every night that there is a full moon."

I watched Petra's shoulders slump before she walked off down the alley, Eirwen following her. My mother put an arm around her shoulder which, surprisingly, the young hunter didn't shrug off. I turned to Bill.

"So what is it with Petra and werewolves?" I asked.

"What do you mean?" The old man rubbed his hand across his eyes. I noticed he looked tired.

"Well, every time that we mention the lycans, she tries to shift the conversation, and when I first mentioned them last night in the café, she looked like she was going to pass out."

Bill sighed as if he was weighing up his response. He reached out and put a hand on my shoulder and for once, I didn't flinch away from him.

"When we train as hunters, each of us goes through various trials. Some of us cope better with situations than others. All of us have differing reactions to the various paranormal beings that we are trained to defend humanity against." I bristled at the comment but he continued.

"What some of us can cope with fine, others cannot. For instance, you saw how easily Petra handled the Church and the vampires. She is one of the most promising young hunters of her generation when it comes to dealing with vampires."

"Oh great!" I chuckled. "Just what I needed to hear."

"Yeah, sorry about that," Bill laughed before turning serious again. "I can hold my own against most vamps, but even in my prime, I think I would have struggled to best you. It would have been a hell of a fight though."

"Wouldn't have happened, Bill," I reassured him. "I'd given up on harming humans decades before you were born."

"Well, be that as it may, vamps I can kill and witches and warlocks I have my protection against. It's the damn succubus that I fall down on," the old guy smiled. "But I can cope with that."

"Ew!" I laughed. "That's a picture I don't want in my head, thank you very much!"

"Petra however, well let's just say that her final test was against a newly turned werewolf," Bill sighed. "It didn't end well for either of them."

"I can relate to that," I told him softly. "I ran into some difficulty with a lycan once so I can understand her fear."

"Is that why you've been nice to her over the last couple of days?"

"What do you mean?" I asked, frowning.

"Normally you're at each other's throats, literally, but I've sensed you holding back when you would normally make snide comments."

"Hey, it's just the new nice Alexander," I laughed, breaking the tone of the conversation. "It's not like I fancy her or anything."

"I didn't say anything about you fancying her," Bill chuckled and, as I walked slightly ahead of him, I heard him mutter under his breath. "Doesn't make it untrue though."

I shook my head to myself. What does the old man know? What a ridiculous idea that he's got. I looked over to where Eirwen was talking softly to Petra. Both of them had blonde hair which was catching Lady Luna's rays, which was contrasting nicely with their black clothing. I shrugged.

"Sun's coming up soon," I said. "I'm gonna get back home and then we'll have to get together and put a plan in place. We're going to need to sweep the more likely places that the wolves can pick off victims."

"I'll have a look at the maps at Uncle Bill's," Petra replied. "We'll come up with at least a dozen spots and we can split into groups and patrol."

"Have a good day's sleep," Bill said as both Eirwen and I leapt into the air, splitting up in mid-flight to go to our respective homes.

"Did Bill find you?" Harry asked as he handed me a coffee. I nodded as I kicked my trainers off and took a seat in the lounge. Harry closed the curtains to stop any early morning sunlight that was breaking over the opposite block of houses from shining in as we talked.

"It was after I'd knocked them all out," I grimaced at the thought that I would have slaughtered four innocents. "They'll have no lasting damage, other than a crashed hand."

"Will they recognise you if they see you again?" my new uncle queried.

"Maybe, but if I avoid them and the sea front for a week or two, it should be okay. I can always cut my hair." I frowned at the thought, remembering the last time I shaved my head. It was as Chlothar was paying respects to Xin-Qa and his household in China in the Fourteenth Century. Chlothar had insisted that all non-warriors paid proper homage to the local tradition and I had complained bitterly for the four months that it took my blonde locks to grow back. It was the middle of winter when we had returned to the castle in Northern France and it was bloody cold!

"So we're back at the drawing board then?" he sighed. "In a way, I was hoping that it was those lads so that we could put an end to it before they killed anyone else."

"Well, it wasn't them so it's back to looking around and patrolling. If it's okay, I'd like to stop by the station and have another look at the files on the Varseys," I asked.

"Why?"

"Something has been bugging me about them and I want to have another look."

"What's been bugging you?"

"I'm not sure," I frowned. "There was something I read in there, I'm sure of it. That's why I want to check the files." I let out a wide yawn as I heard the beginning of a late dawn chorus. I couldn't believe that some birds stayed behind in the colder north of England rather than following their cousins to warmer climates.

"Well, it looks like you need to hit the hay," Harry told me, holding his hand out. I took it and pulled myself up, handing him the now empty coffee cup. I went to my room, got into bed, pulling the drapes securely round and before my head even hit the pillow, I had succumbed to the daysleep.

"Alexander? Is that you?" a sweet voice whispered through the woods.

"Yes, my Lady," I giggled quietly as I stepped out from behind a tree. "Did you manage to give your guards the slip?"

"I did, but it will not be long before they find me so we don't have much time," Lady Catherine sighed. She flicked back her long blonde hair which allowed the evening dusk to frame her alabaster white skin.

"You look beautiful tonight," I stammered out, patting down my crumpled doublet. It was a present for my fourteenth birthday, albeit a hand-me-down from Jakob, a boy a year older than me who's family lived two houses down. I held out the single white lily that I had found by the river.

"You mean I normally look frightful?" she asked, a smile playing on her lips as she watched me fluster an apology. She took the flower remarking on how nice it was.

"If your father ever finds out about you meeting me, my Lady," I started but she placed a finger on my lips to silence me.

"My father will do whatever I ask him," she whispered as she moved her body close to mine. My heart beat skipped as I smelled the fresh scent of an exotic soap on her. "If you want me to, I will ask him to make you a squire so that you can move into the castle."

"But my Lady, my family need me," I sighed. "My mother has just had a new baby so I have to earn my keep and help my step-father with the herds."

"A new baby! Oh how wonderful!" Catherine hugged me close. "Is it a boy or a girl?"

"A boy," I smiled as the image of the baby flashed in my mind. "I have a brother."

"What's his name?"

"Coachuhhar," I told her. "It's Celtic for being wise or something. My stepfather tried to explain it."

"I cannot wait until I have children of my own," Catherine said. "I also can't wait until I start practicing to have children."

I flushed red, knowing exactly what she meant. For the last three weeks, we had been sneaking away from our respective homes to meet at the edge of the woods. To begin with, it was just to sit and talk, Catherine telling me about life in the castle and she pressed me for details of being a sheepherder, and of living in the village. We had held hands as we walked around the small lake, the new moon waxing towards fullness as the days progressed until finally, tonight, she turned to me as we looked across the lake.

"Alexander," she started. "Most boys would already have kissed and had their hands all over me by now. Do you not find me attractive?"

"My Lady, you are the most beautiful woman that I have ever seen," I blushed. "You are also noble born, whereas I am but a serf and so it wouldn't be proper for me to try things like that. Your father would have me beaten."

"My father isn't here, Alexander," Catherine smiled. I felt my knees weaken and my body react to her. She leaned into me and our lips met for a moment. She pulled away to look into my eyes. I could see my reflection in her blue eyes and gave in to her desires. I kissed her again, our arms encircling each other's' bodies and as the rays of the full moon hit the glade, I wondered if life could be any more perfect.

I felt Catherine stiffen in my grip and as I broke the kiss, pulling away slightly to make sure that she was okay, I saw her face grimace in pain.

"Are you okay, Catherine?" I asked, a hint of panic in my voice.

"I don't know, Alexander. There's something wrong!" she cried. I held her head in my hands but let out a gasp as I watched her eyes widen, the colour of her irises changing from the pale blue to a dark brown.

"BOY! Get away from her!" I heard a deep voice behind me. I span around and saw five men standing on the edge of the lake. They all had wicked looking swords in their hands.

"NO!" I shouted back. "I'll not let you hurt her."

"She isn't what you think, boy. Now move!" the taller of the five took a step forward before the man at the rear placed a hand on his arm.

"Captain Paulinos, hold for a moment," the man said. I could feel the strength of command in his voice as the warrior held his ground.

"Sire, we must destroy the beast before it turns," Captain Paulinos argued.

"There are guards coming from the castle, Sire," a second warrior added.

"We cannot be seen," the leader of them explained. "Our presence in this range must be undetected."

I heard the heavy footsteps of the Earl's guards approaching and let out a sigh of relief. They would protect the Lady Catherine from these intruders but as I turned to her to let her know that she was safe, I watched in horror as she dropped to the ground.

"She's turning, sire," the Captain hissed and I felt myself flung to the side. I wondered how he had covered the forty yards in an instant but as my head struck a tree stump, I decided that the pain in my head was more of a concern.

"NO!" I yelled as I saw him raise his sword and I flung myself at him, knocking him to the side as his blade fell, slicing through empty air.

"Damn you boy, you know not what you are protecting," he snarled at me.

"I'm protecting my Lady," I shouted back, trying to lead the guards towards us. My head was throbbing and I felt my vision blurring slightly but as I looked down at Catherine, I realised that I must have hit my head harder than I thought. Mixed in with the image of her face was that of an animal. Her jaw had elongated and I could see her hair darkening.

"Get away from her, boy," the one that they had referred to as their sire hissed at me, just as three of the Earl's guards rushed into the glade. "Let us destroy the beast before it's too late."

"Stay away from our Lady," the guard who had warned me previously shouted. I span and tried to place myself in between Catherine and danger but as he lunged his sword towards the dark haired leader of the men, I stumbled into their path and I felt my stomach puncture.

I looked down as my brain tried to disconnect itself from the pain now coursing through my body and my mouth dropped open as I saw at least five inches of steel had been pushed inside my body. I lifted my head and looked the guard in the eyes, seeing regret in his as he realised that he had stabbed me instead of the attackers.

Pain wrecked my thoughts as he pulled his sword out of my stomach and I collapsed onto the floor, my hands desperately trying to hold my guts inside my body where they belonged. I could feel myself floating as darkness began to settle in my brain. A strange howl of an animal echoed in my ears before the shouts of men dying drowned it out. A loud animalistic yelp silenced the glade before I heard a grunt of satisfaction.

"The beast is dead," the leader said, a confidence in his voice.

"Her guards are also disposed of, my sire," another said. "Our presence here will be kept secret."

I tried to remain quiet, but as I shifted slightly, I let out a cry of pain through my clenched teeth.

"What of the boy?" the one that they called Captain asked. "He fought bravely defending who he thought was a Lady. He doesn't deserve to die in agony." I looked up at him and again, my eyes must have been deceiving me as the man looked as though he had fangs.

"Please sir, don't kill me," I begged. Thoughts of my family flashed through my mind as I wondered how they would cope without my help.

"I can save you, boy, but it will mean you can never return to your family," the leader told me. I turned my head in surprise as he had been on the far side of the glade. Now, he was holding my stomach. I looked at him and gasped at the bright red glow of his eyes.

"But my family need me, sir," I tried to explain, but as I finished speaking, a blood splatter cough erupted from my mouth.

"You are dying, boy. I can end it quickly or I can save you. The choice is yours," the man said.

"Is this wise?" the Captain asked.

"The boy has skills. I think he could be a fine bodyguard."

"Please sir. Save me!" I begged. My vision was blurring.

"You will serve me?" the man asked.

"Yes sir, if you will pay my family," I tried my luck.

"That I will, boy. What is your name?"

"Alexander. Alexander of Farrow's Haven, sir," I stammered out.

"Well, Alexander of Farrow's Haven, you are now part of the House of Chlothar," the man smiled before his mouth opened into a horrifying vision of fangs. I tried to struggle, to get away from him as his mouth descended onto my neck. Pain hit my body as I felt his teeth pierce the skin, just above my shoulder. My stomach cramped as I felt the flow of blood weaken to a dribble before the whole of my body felt like it was being burned from the inside.

"Carry him," Chlothar commanded. "The venom will disable him for two days and we need to be gone before the beast's pack comes looking."

I felt myself being lifted by the Captain and I was thrown over his shoulder. The ground seemed to shrink away from me and I succumbed to unconsciousness as the wind whistled through my hair.

Chapter Ten

"Alex? Are you okay?"

I jerked awake, sweat trickling down my brow. Y'cart was holding a cloth to my head, while Eirwen and Harry were looking on with worried eyes. I was still in my room, but I could tell that there was something amiss.

"What time is it? What's happened?" I asked, trying to sit up only to be held back by the witch's firm grip.

"You were shouting out in your sleep again," Harry explained. "This sounded worse than any of your other dreams and when you started talking about a werewolf, I called Eirwen."

"It sounded like you were remembering the night you met Chlothar," Eirwen said softly. "The night that he turned you."

"I remembered more than I had before," I frowned. "Catherine. I was with Catherine and I thought that the guard had stabbed me because of me being with her."

"But?"

"But I had just gotten in his way as I was protecting her from Chlothar. But I shouldn't have been." I sat up, the memory of pain in my stomach making me grimace. "She was a lycan."

"No wonder you have this hatred for them," Harry frowned. "If your first love was really a werewolf, that would screw with anyone's head."

"Maybe," I huffed. I rubbed my stomach, trying to ease the pain that I felt. It didn't feel right that I could bring my pain from my nightmare into reality, but even seven hundred years since gaining my first power, the fact was that I was still learning new tricks. That was something that I could look into, after we'd dealt with these lycans of course.

"Come on, you may as well get up if you want to go through the files at the station," Harry told me. "We'll see you downstairs."

I watched as they filed out, Eirwen automatically assuming the front, but I had to smile as Harry held the door for Y'cart to walk through. I had to try to filter out my empathic powers whenever they were both in the same room as me as the feelings that my pretend uncle had for the witch were only increasing by the day.

I shrugged off the thoughts of love and romance, wondering if the potential blossoming relationship between Harry and Y'cart was playing tricks on my mind while I was asleep. I hadn't thought about Lady Catherine in a couple of hundred years so why had I now had two dreams in the last three nights?

As I walked into the kitchen, I sensed Eirwen's anxiety about tonight's full moon. However, I was slightly distracted by the sudden hush between Harry and Y'cart as I reached for the always full coffee jug.

"So do you have any idea who the lycans could be?" I asked my mother figure, ignoring the pair of humans for now.

"No, and that's what's worrying me," Eirwen replied. "The moon is due up in around an hour and they will be on the hunt."

"Why don't you go on a scout and I'll come and join you after I've been to the station?" I suggested. "But keep it quiet from Bill and Petra."

"Keep what quiet from us?" I groaned as I heard the sixteen year old huntress walking into the kitchen.

"Alex thinks that it would be better if you two wait until we find out who the lycans are," Y'cart tried to play the peacekeeper.

"I'm off to the station," I announced before Petra had a chance to retort. "Are you coming, Uncle Harry?"

I turned and walked past the pair of hunters, nodding at Bill, who's eyes were a mystery to me. There was a mix of gratitude and surprise in them. I watched as Harry bade a farewell to the witch before following me out of the kitchen. As we waited for the elevator to ascend from the underground car park, I turned back to him.

"You know that it won't work?"

"What won't?" he asked. "The potion? Eirwen has every faith in Y'cart and so do I."

"No, I don't give a damn about the potion," I sighed. Somehow, despite all of my reservations, all of my defences, I had succumbed. "I mean you and Y'cart."

"What do you mean, Y'cart and me?" I could hear the nervousness in his voice.

"She's over six hundred years old and is going to live for another few hundred. There's nothing that can be done to extend your life so any romance between you is going to be just a flicker in her life."

"Why do you suddenly care about Y'cart's feelings?" he chuckled and we stepped to one side as the door opened to avoid being barged over by two small hurricanes.

"ALEX! You wanna come and play on my console?" the older of the two boys asked.

"I'm sorry Petey, but I need to go and help Uncle Harry at the police station," I explained, dropping to one knee so that I was in eye line with the boy. "How about I come by in a few days when it's the weekend and we can stay up all night playing?"

"Can we Mum? Puh-leeaze?" the boy dragged out the plea for a few seconds longer than his mother could bear.

"I'm sure we can arrange that," Linda smiled, before she leaned towards me. "He thinks the world of you, and so I do I for spending time with the boys."

"No problem," I shrugged. "I remember being a kid." I got a nudge from Harry.

"Linda, do me a favour. Keep the boys and yourself inside for the next few nights," Harry said. "We don't think there is a big problem, but some of the public have been reporting sights of an animal over at Marton Mere."

"An animal? What kind?" she asked, pulling her youngest to her.

"It's nothing to worry about, I'm sure, but I would prefer you to be safe than sorry," my uncle replied. "We've got to go, sorry. I'll pop round in the morning for a coffee."

We stepped into the elevator and waved goodbye to the two boys as the doors closed.

"They've changed a lot since you moved in," Harry nodded in the direction of the boys.

"They just needed a little guidance and distraction," I replied. "Linda was being overwhelmed by them."

"Well, they're good for you as well," he added.

I decided to get back to the topic of our original conversation.

"I don't care about Y'cart's feelings," I started, a little gnaw in my mind telling me that wasn't strictly true. "I don't want to see you get hurt in a few years when she moves on."

"So it's my feelings you're worried about?" Harry smiled. I shrugged, not wanting to put into words the fact that I'd let him get past my defences. In the last couple of months, he had acted like a father would, albeit we played the role of uncle and nephew and I realised that he was the first person in over one and a half centuries that actually gave a damn if I was okay. I found myself growing attached to him, to care for him and I didn't want any further hardship to befall him. Losing a son is enough in my book.

The ride to the station was peaceful. Most of the revellers had forgone their evening wanderings as a bitterly cold wind blew in from the north. As we pulled up in the car park, he turned to me.

"Shit. You might need to have your glimmer thingy ready," he said.

"Why? Most of the night duty officers know me so there isn't normally a problem."

"The new Chief Superintendent is here," Harry pointed to a brand new Jaguar parked in the disabled bay.

I frowned at his choice of parking, remembering that the man seemed able enough. As we headed through the front desk, I nodded and smiled at Sargent Macaulay, a petite brunette whose smile made my knees wobble for some reason. The fact that she was a black belt in ju-jitsu warned off any unwelcome admirers and for me, just added to the young lady's charm.

"The new Chief's in with the DCI, Harry," she said as he pressed the buttons on the vending machine. A plastic cup fell onto the floor as the machine emptied its contents into the drip tray. He flashed me an unhappy look as I sniggered.

"It tastes like crap, Uncle Harry," I laughed. "Get some water and then we can go to the coffee shop… or Sargent Macaulay could make you one from her tin of filter beans that she's got hidden behind the desk."

"How do you know about that, Alex?" she asked, her guilty eyes flashing downwards.

"I can smell your cup from here," I smiled. "It smells lovely by the way."

"This one has gotten himself addicted to strong coffee," Harry grabbed me by the shoulders and started to frog march me past the desk, and the filter coffee! "See you in a while, Sargent."

"But, but… I was about to get a decent cup Uncle Harry," I whined as we walked away from the front desk to the sound of chuckles from Sargent Macaulay and I sat heavily on the spare chair by Harry's desk.

"Evening Harry," Detective Jackson mumbled and he nodded to me. His eyes had rings of black underneath them.

"Hello Sammy, you look terrible," Harry replied, taking his own seat and pulled a folder from his inbox.

"The little one is crying continuously through the day," Harry's partner moaned. "I'm hardly getting any sleep at all."

"Just before you're trying to put him down, give him a warm bath laced with lavender," I suggested without thinking as I turned to Harry's computer. I keyed in his log on, much to Harry's frustration. He regularly changed his password but what he didn't realise was that as he typed, he pressed those keys a little firmer than when he was using the computer normally. It was then just a process of simple elimination to put the letters into a word.

"Will that work?" Detective Jackson asked. "I've considered giving him a shot of whiskey as that's what my old man used to give me."

"Trust me, lavender is much better for him," I explained. "And it saves your whiskey for the proper drinkers." I grinned as I pulled up the files on the Varseys.

"So what do you think you missed?" Harry asked as he looked over my shoulder.

"Just something about where he worked," I replied as I pulled up the file onto the screen. I scrolled to the personal details of Leo Varsey and there it was. I let out a soft sigh of frustration and ground my teeth together.

"What is it, Alex? What did you find?"

"Leo Varsey worked as a sales representative for an electronics manufacturer." Harry looked at me with a question in his eyes. "He worked for the company owned by Ian Norris."

"The same Ian Norris who has just moved here?" Detective Jackson asked, his eyes perking up slightly. "He was free with his bar tab at the hotel the other night," the detective rubbed his head in remembrance. "I think it was the vodka that killed me."

"That and the Sambuca," I giggled.

"Sambuca? Oh Christ, no wonder I was ill," he groaned.

"Anyway, if Mr Varsey worked for Ian Norris, that gives us a link," I said.

"A link to what?" Detective Jackson asked. I forgot that he wasn't 'in' on our secret world and nearly blurted out more than he should know. "I thought that they were killed by an animal or something."

"Something is more likely than an animal," I muttered under my breath.

"But the records show that the Norris's didn't relocate here until after the Varseys were killed," Harry pointed out.

"That's the only confusing thing about this," I agreed. "But it does put them straight back as number one suspects in my book."

"Why would Ian Norris want to kill his sales rep?" Detective Jackson queried, looking confused. I turned to Harry, looking for a way out of answering with the truth.

"Who said anything about Ian Norris being a murderer?" A deep voice echoed across the room, silencing the department. I turned and saw the Chief Superintendent striding across to Harry and Sammy's desks, with DCI Bach in tow.

"Um, it's just a theory that we're working on, Chief," Harry started.

"Well it's a theory that you can disregard immediately," the Chief hissed. "Ian Norris is a fine upstanding member of our community and has created a lot of much needed jobs. If I hear anyone in this department spreading malicious gossip about him or his family, they will find themselves back walking the beat. DO I MAKE MYSELF CLEAR?"

There were a few mumbled 'Yes Chiefs' before the man turned and noticed me.

"What is a kid doing in here?" he demanded. I noticed his nostrils flaring and his eyes seemed to fix on me in a way that I didn't care for. For a moment, I felt like I was a lamb or a deer, caught in the sight of a predator before my vampire strength made itself known to me. This was just a human, albeit a man with political power but he was no physical threat to me.

"This is Detective Shepherd's nephew, Alex," DCI Bach interjected. "He has been very helpful with some of our cases as he sees things that other people don't."

"What do you mean?" the Chief asked.

"He's a genius, is what the DCI means, guv," Detective Jackson smiled. "He can read a set of files and make connections that we miss."

"Well that might be true, but kids shouldn't be looking at dead bodies," the Chief said. "In fact, he really shouldn't be in here at all."

"I was just leaving," I announced. "I'll see you at home, Uncle Harry. Nice seeing you again Detective and make sure you use that lavender."

"I'll walk you out," Harry said before the Chief put his hand on my shoulder

"You've got work to do. I was leaving anyway so I can drop him off if he tells me the way."

I stiffened as the man touched me. The smell was too intense for me to have any doubts. I was wrong when I thought that Chief Superintendent Leighton was no physical threat to me. As he led me away, Harry not having any reason to counter the Chief's suggestion, I cast a quick glance back at him. Harry's eyes widened as he saw my momentary fear flashing in my eyes.

I had found one of the lycans and it was Blackpool's newly appointed Chief Superintendent.

Michael Andrews

Chapter Eleven

I allowed him to walk me through the front office, my mind reeling at the possibilities of what this meant. Not only was he the top policeman in the area, but he also held a lot of political sway due to his position. This opened up anyone in power to being a member of his pack.

That was the thing about lycans. They craved power in both their wolf form as well as their human form. There had been rumours of in-pack fighting for centuries as each wolf tried to become the alpha, or at least the beta wolf and this fed over into human form. With Greg Leighton being in such a dominant position in the police force, he had to be in the upper hierarchy of his pack. He pointed me in the direction of his Jaguar and I was caught in two minds whether to go along with the pretence or not. After all, he could hardly change into a wolf while driving, could he?

"Get in son," he told me. "I'll soon have you home. We don't want a lad like you walking the streets getting mugged or anything now do we?"

"No sir," I replied politely and opened the door. I slipped into the passenger seat and fastened my seat belt. If I turned vamp, the safety strap wouldn't have the strength to hold me so I had no fears of being trapped.

He reversed out of the parking bay, narrowly missing a cyclist who turned to swear at him before the Chief started slowly down the road, picking up speed as we weaved our way through the roads of the town centre.

I had to fight to remain in control of myself as the stench of lupine sweat reeked from every pore on his body as his eyes flicked from the road, to me and up to the now visible full moon, shining down on Blackpool. My phone buzzed in my pocket and I pulled it out, ignoring his stare.

'Are you okay?' was the text from Harry.

I quickly thumbed back, *'I'm fine. Tell Eirwen to get to the nature reserve. It's him.'*

I knew that I was taking a risk telling Harry that CS Leighton was a lycan as he was more prone to come after us himself rather than leave it to Eirwen and me but I hoped that he would see sense.

"So where do you live?" the big guy asked me.

"Not far," I lied. "It's just along here, turn left and then down, just past the reserve."

"I thought that Detective Shepherd lived on the other side of town for some reason," he said. I saw him cast a sideways glance at me and if I didn't know better, I could swore he licked his lips.

"He moved a while ago," I tried it on. "It was just after the trouble he had."

"Oh yes, his son running away like that. It must be terrible."

I could feel the coldness in his voice, but my mind was distracted as we pulled into the car park of the nature reserve. If I wasn't a vampire, then I would have been frightened but, as I turned to him, I tried to play the scared kid.

"Why are we stopping here, sir?" I asked. "Uncle Harry's house is still another half a mile away."

"I've got a cramp in my leg, boy," the Chief replied. "I just need to stretch it out. Come outside for a moment while I walk it off."

I watched him get out of the car and shrugged and followed him as he walked to the path leading into the trees. He made a show of seeing something further down the path and beckoned me to follow him to investigate. I hid the smile on my face at his efforts to lead me away from the car park and from the sight of any passing car.

"What have you seen, Mr Leighton?" I asked.
"I was sure that I saw someone on the path," he lied. I could feel confidence oozing from him and readied myself. "They must have crawled into the trees. Come and help me look."
"Are you sure? I mean, that animal is supposed to be around here."
"Don't worry about that," he replied. "It's quite safe."

I followed him off the path and into darkness. The Chief slowed and allowed me to pass him before I heard the unmistakeable sound of a low growl. I turned and saw the Chief stood stock still. Just off to the side was the large form of a wolf, jet black with burning red eyes that were fixed on me. This wasn't how I planned things to happen. I had expected it just to be the Chief but I had badly misjudged things.

"Here he is, as promised," the Chief said to the wolf.

The general misconception of many was that, when a lycan went wolf, they turned fully into an animal. However, the way that the wolf turned its attention from me to the Chief and back again proved that they kept their human reasoning, just like we vampires did when we shape shifted.

The wolf growled at him and I saw a hesitant look spread over onto his face. I could sense a tinge of fear in the man and as I tried to open my mind to the wolf, an overwhelming surge of power rocked my body. This unexpected wolf wasn't just a pack member, this was the Alpha.

"I was instructed to bring an easy kill to start the cycle," the Chief seemed to whine. His standing was obviously less than I previously thought, if he was just a herder. The wolf shifted on its haunches and bared its fangs at the man who took a step back.

"You never said anything about avoiding this kid. How would I know not to bring this one in particular?" He flashed a look over at me, probably expecting me to be cowering in fear but with adrenaline beginning to kick in, I puffed out my chest.

"You won't find me such an easy kill, lycan scum," I hissed. Whilst still wondering about his comments, I still expected a fight so I allowed my nails to grow, wishing that I had my sword at my side. However, I was more than comfortable fighting with tooth and claw, my preferred style much to Captain Paulinos' displeasure.

My simple statement certainly got the Alpha's attention as it started a slow circle of me. I heard a groan of pain and while I kept my main focus on the wolf, I saw the Chief shed his shirt out of the corner of my eye. Hair was growing all over his body and as he held up a hand, I saw it stretch and twist into a large, fur covered paw. I was fascinated. I had never seen a true transformation before, as vampires simply fixed the shape of the animal in our minds and willed out the change. It was mainly instantaneous, taking mere seconds as our bodies took on the change. It looked like a lycan didn't have that power, instead the moon's power was the architect of their transformation.

I felt pain in my arm and realised that I had become distracted by the Chief's shifting and had taken my eyes off the wolf. The Alpha had taken its opportunity and had bitten me as it darted past me. It sat down, watching me as blood dripped from my arm and I clenched my teeth as I felt venom enter my veins. Instinct kicked in as I realised that the beast wasn't trying to kill me. Instead, it was trying to turn me. The reasoning I could work out later. For now, I had to stop the venom and get out alive as once the wolf realised what I was, it would be a fight to the death.

I gritted my teeth and sweat dribbled down my brow as I forced the blood through my veins at a faster than normal pace. I could feel the venom racing around my body but I knew that once it reached my heart, my healing process would cleanse it from my system as vampire antibodies released themselves to attack.

A howl to my left caused me to stumble slightly and, as I reached out to steady myself on the nearest tree, I saw that the Chief had now fully transformed and two full grown werewolves were now staring me down. All communication with them was now impossible and the only way out would be to flee, or to fight.

My vision began to shift spectrums as infra-red and the eerie green of night vision flickered with my normal sight, making me the ultimate predator. Lycans could only use their one vision, although their hearing was better than ours so it was always a close battle whenever our two species fought. I doubled in pain as I felt the lycan venom entered my heart, crying out as it penetrated each of the chambers before beginning the cycle around my body. I could hear a low, satisfied growl from the Alpha as I clutched the tree to remain on my feet, my teeth gritting in agony as I finally felt my antibodies begin their battle with the werewolf disease.

Michael Andrews

"ALEX!" I heard Harry's shout from the path and looked up to see him running through the undergrowth, stopping up short at the sight of the two wolves.

"Harry, stay back," I hissed. "They'll kill you given the chance."

"They can try," he snarled. "But I'm not leaving you undefended. Come on you animals, you'll have to get through me if you want him."

I cursed the length of time it was taking my body to recover. Despite the feed that I'd had, I assumed that, as it was an Alpha's bite, it was taking my body longer to fight off the infection. I heard a rustle of leaves and saw the Chief's wolf form leap at Harry, his fangs bared and ready to bite. I stumbled forwards as quickly as I could and managed to push Harry over, just as the wolf sailed past, snapping at thin air.

It landed and turned, staring at me with cold, black eyes. I shook myself, finally ridding myself of the venom when I was hit hard from behind. I span in mid-air, watching in transfixed horror as Harry's body crumpled to the ground under the attack of the Alpha. His arms were in front of his face as the wolf tried to maul him and I let out a string of curses as I slammed into the trunk of a tree.

I jumped to my feet, ready to leap at the Alpha before a blur of blonde shot past me, knocking the wolf away from Harry.

"Eirwen, there's two of them!" I called out as she landed, rolling away from the Alpha and into a crouched defensive posture.

"You get the other, I'll take this one," she instructed me.

I turned just in time to dodge the leap of the Chief, the wolf sailing past my quick reaction swerve and as he landed, I jumped, landing on his back. I wrapped my arms

106

around his neck, trying to find a grip but his fur was too slick for me to hold on.

He twisted, throwing me from his back and I landed heavily on an upturned bolder. My head spun as it hit the stone face first and I felt blood in my mouth from my now broken nose. I tried to turn and stand but my knees wobbled underneath me and I stumbled back to the grassy floor.

"Stay away from him!" Harry growled at the wolf and raised his gun, firing shot after shot into the body of the animal.

"Tell me they're silver," I whispered out, praying that Harry knew his lore but it was obvious as the Chief turned to him that he was unaffected by the bullets.

The beast leapt at him once more, Harry reaching out with his arms almost in an embrace, but as their bodies collided, Harry turned his waist and threw the wolf to the ground. I almost crowed in appreciation of the move when I heard a twang of a crossbow. The whistle of a bolt hummed out through the night air before the thud of impact sent the Chief flying backwards ten feet.

"Harry? Are you okay?" Bill's voice echoed and I turned to see the two hunters entering the wooded area.

"Just about," my uncle groaned, rubbing his side. "Where are Alex and Eirwen?"

"Alex is here," Petra said as she crouched down by my side. I must have hit my head harder than I thought as I was sure I saw a look of concern within her expression. "Stay down for a moment and let us do our job."

"I'm okay," I replied but as I sat up, the light headedness returned. "Where's the wolf?"

"It ran off over in that direction," Bill told us as he helped Harry to his feet. I could see a red stain on his side which appeared to be getting larger by the minute.

"I need to help Eirwen," I growled and forced myself to stand. "She's fighting the Alpha."

"We'll go and help," Petra insisted. "You're too unsteady on your feet."

"I'm okay, but Harry stays, he's injured," I said and nodded to Bill.

"I'll help him back to his car," the old man said. "Be careful you two."

"Come on," I said to the young hunter. "I can sense Eirwen in that direction."

The two of us picked our way through some broken bushes and as we crept along, I felt a sense of urgency growing inside of me. Fear permutated through my empathic feelings but as I looked at Petra, her face was a mask of steely determination. It wasn't coming from her but I began to get a sense of panic. I picked up my pace, grinding my teeth as Petra struggled to keep up with me before I grabbed her waist.

"Hold on to me," I told her. "We need to find her now."

"If you hold me through my arm, I can keep my crossbow aimed," Petra replied.

It seemed like a plan and, within seconds, we were speeding through the woods. I heard a cry of pain. A cry of pain from a woman and my mind reeled as the pain hit my own senses. I staggered to a halt as my vision blurred, almost colliding with a tree and I stumbled to the ground, twisting my body so that it shielded Petra from any injury as we fell. We rolled over, Petra crouching, crossbow ready as she scanned the surroundings.

Another cry of distress sounded through the branches, this time an animalistic growl of agony and I pinpointed their position some yards away from us. I motioned Petra to follow on silent feet and, as I peered around the tree, my heart constricted in panic and fear.

The Alpha wolf was limping away from the small clearing, its front left leg dragging painfully as it hobbled away, casting swift glances behind. The Chief's wolf form was standing over the prone body of Eirwen, her face a crumpled grimace of blood and fur. Her eyes flashed from the wolf to me, back to the wolf before taking one last look in my direction.

My heart stopped. My vision narrowed onto the sharp teeth outlined by dark fur as they fell, ripping open the lily white neck of my former mother figure. I barely heard the twang of Petra's crossbow as a sliver arrow streaked through the air, burying itself into the heart of the wolf, propelling it away from Eirwen's body.

My body changed instantly. There was no gradual push from myself. I flew across the clearing, covering the distance between myself and the Chief in a fraction of a second. My fangs were extended and as I grabbed the badly injured lycan, I wrapped my arms around its neck and pulled it to an angle where I could get a clear bite at its throat.

I tasted fur as my lengthened incisors ripped into the flesh of the wolf, the warm flow of blood causing a slight steam to rise as I tore away fur, meat and veins, not caring to feed... just to kill. The Chief struggled underneath me, trying desperately to escape. His yowls of pain, mixed in with calls for help being unanswered by the escaping Alpha quietened as the spurts of scarlet blood erupted from the savaging that I was inflicting.

I could hear a voice, a sweet voice calling my name, pleading with me to stop my vicious assault on the now limp form and I pulled back, spitting to discard the pieces of flesh in my mouth. I rocked on my haunches, gazing at the mess that I had made of the beast but as a hand touched my shoulder, I span ready to attack once more.

"Alexander... it's me!" The DCI yelped, jumping backwards out of reach of my clawed hand. The distressed look on her face was enough to bring me out of my attack and I refocused, purging the adrenaline from my body. My vision swam for a moment as it switched back to normal vision and, as I stood, I saw the look of awe tinged with horror on the face of Petra.

"How's Eirwen?" I begged DCI Bach, not wanting to hear the reply but already I could sense an overwhelming crushing weight on her mind.

"She's gone, Alexander," the DCI sobbed finally, wiping her eyes. "I followed Harry as soon as I heard him call Eirwen but we're too late."

"She can't be gone," I insisted. "She's too strong for a wolf."

"Alex… there were two of them, one of them an Alpha," Petra said softly, edging towards me, her crossbow not pointing at me, but the threat was there all the same. It didn't need my empathic powers to sense her wariness of me.

"I'm not going to attack you, Petra," I sighed. "I'm fully in control of myself."

I walked the short few steps to Eirwen's body, fighting back the tears that threatened to spill from my soul. Her throat had been torn open by the bites of the wolves, blood splatters covering the front of her white blouse. I could see that her spine had been shattered, the cerebral cortex ripped apart, ending her eight hundred year life. My fists clenched at the thought that she was no longer with us, with me. I had lost my mother figure for the second time in my life.

I turned back towards the wolf that I had killed, only to see that it had reverted back into human form and a very naked dead Chief Leighton lay in front of us. Petra's crossbow bolt still protruded from his side and his throat was in a similar state to that of Eirwen's.

"I didn't realise that they did that," Petra whispered as she came to stand next to me, looking down at the corpse. "What are we going to do with the body?"

"We can't just get rid of it," I replied. "He was too prominent in human life for that. What do you suggest?" I turned to the DCI who I saw struggling to stand upright.

"Are you okay, Vanessa?" Petra asked. Insight hit me square in the eyes.

"It's the bond link," I hissed. "It's now broken and unless she's strong enough, it will kill her."

"Isn't there anything we can do?" the young hunter urged.

"The links can be removed," I started, but as Petra's eyes brightened, I had to extinguish that hope. "But not by me. I do not have the skill or power."

"Well, what are we going to do?" Petra asked, hesitation in her voice. I could tell that she wanted to take charge, but having seen me in full vampire attack mode, I sensed she was waiting for me to make the decisions.

"Why don't you help Vanessa back to your uncle's car and I'll bring the Chief's body," I told her. "Then I'll come back for Eirwen's."

With the decision made, I watched as the two blondes walked into the trees, the younger supporting the older and I turned back to the two corpses. Ignoring the dead Chief Superintendent for now, I crumpled at the side of Eirwen's body. Tears finally flooded from my eyes as I grieved for the loss of the woman who had been my mother for centuries.

The woods quietened as if sharing in my grief but, as the moments stretched, I knew that if I didn't get back to the cars soon, they would come looking for me. I wiped my tear stained face, not wanting humans to see my moment of weakness before I picked up the Chief's body. Leaping into the air, I flew the half mile back to the car park, landing next to Bill's car. We loaded the body into the trunk of his car before Harry turned to me.

"I'll take his car and drive it back to his house," Harry suggested. "He's a widower so there will be no-one there and then we can decided later what to do. Petra, can you drive?"

"Course I can," she replied. "It's part of our training."

"Well, you take my car and follow your uncle back to our houses and we'll see you back there."

"What about Alex?" she asked, looking at me as I stood quietly to one side. Concern was etched on her face which I shook off.

"I'm going to take Eirwen back to Y'cart's house and talk to her about what we can do for the DCI," I replied.

"I'm fine," Vanessa announced suddenly, getting up out of Bill's car. "It still hurts like crap, but I'm a stubborn old coot who's not going to let this take her down."

"That's a relief," Harry breathed a loud sigh of relief. "Is there anything you need?"

"No, I'll be fine. Alex, go and get my Lady's body and I'll meet you at Y'cart's."

Chapter Twelve

I landed in Y'cart's back garden, Eirwen's limp body in my arms. Once again tears threatened to spill from my eyes and I had to fight to keep control of my emotions as the witch rushed through the kitchen door, stopping a step away from me. She had no problem letting her emotions show as she sobbed, reaching out a hand to touch her mistress's face. I had wrapped my hoodie around Eirwen's upper body to hide the damage that Chief Leighton had inflicted.

"I can't believe she's gone," Y'cart cried, as she walked by my side as I carried Eirwen inside.

"We got one of them and injured the Alpha as well," I said softly, hoping that she would find some comfort in knowing that we scored our own small victory.

I took Eirwen upstairs and laid her on a bed, covering her with a sheet before heading back downstairs. Harry was pulling up in his car and the four humans got out and walked into the house. DCI Bach immediately embraced Y'cart, sharing their grief at the loss of the vampire who had come into their lives.

"Are you okay, kiddo?" Harry asked me. I flashed a look at him, refusing to meet his eyes and nodded. I refused to give in to my grief in front of them.

"What are we going to do with the body?" Bill asked.

"I've taken her upstairs," I sighed. "We can give her a fitting send off once we've dealt with the rest of the pack."

"That's good, but I actually meant CS Leighton," the old hunter replied.

No-one answered and I looked up, trying to force myself to put my own sorrow to one side. They were all looking at me for a decision and I snapped at them.

"Why are you looking at me for answers?" I shouted. "I'm not a leader, I'm just a bodyguard!"

"Hey, take it easy," Petra started. I stopped her with a look but she pushed on anyway. Pulling me to one side, she said, "Y'cart and Vanessa can't lead us because they're too upset and Uncle Bill has never faced a werewolf pack before. I'm only just out of training and your Uncle Harry only found out about the real world three months ago."

"And your point is?"

"My point is, Alexander, like it or not you are the most experienced and the most knowledgeable of all of us," she explained. "I've been watching you and when you know what to do, you're decisive and take action regardless of the consequences. Unfortunately this time, there was a consequence that affects you, but you have to stay focused on the bigger picture. You can grieve later."

"I've known Eirwen for over eight centuries," I heard the slight hitch in my voice. "While she wasn't my real mother, she has been the closest thing to it for most of that time. I can't just shake off her death and pretend that nothing is wrong."

"No-one expects you to. Everyone can make mistakes and we know that you're not perfect. But you're still our best hope for stopping these lycans before they kill again. Just, well, just don't be afraid to ask for help as well. You don't have to make all of the decisions on your own. Just be the authoritive voice that you were when Beddows van Hightinger was in town."

"When did you get so smart and tactful?" I flashed a weak grin at her.

"When I grew up. I'm sorry I was so horrible to you before. All that I saw was the vampire that I was trained to hate, not the actual person that you are. My uncle has taught me about the grey in the world."

"So what do *you* think we should do with the Chief's body?" I asked, putting her on the spot.

"Well, we can't hide the ripped throat or the hole in his side where my bolt got him," she started. "I suggest stabbing him with a knife to disguise the puncture wound and using the same knife to make it look like his throat was cut."

"Then we can dump his body in a back street and pretend he's been killed during a mugging?" I queried.

"Exactly," she smiled. "We can send a message to The Comitia to get a patsy to take the fall. It's been done in the past."

"That I'd like to hear about," I started but we were interrupted by the sound of DCI Bach's shriek.

"OH MY GOD! JASON!" she cried into her phone.

I cursed, several times. I had forgotten about the ten year old boy who was also bonded to Eirwen. While Vanessa was, in her own words, stubborn enough to have the mental strength to survive the death of her mistress, there was no way that the young boy would.

"If you take me to him, I can make it painless," Y'cart announced.

"No," I hissed. "We're not killing him." I looked around at her shelves. "Do you have the ingredients of Endless Sleep?"

"Yes, but…"

"But nothing," I scowled. "You get the potion ready and I'll bring the boy here. We'll put him to sleep while we work something out."

I watched Petra smirk as Y'cart stared at me for a moment before turning and started to pick jars from her shelves. The huntress spoke to Vanessa for a moment before turning back to me.

"Vanessa will call her sister and brother in law back and let them know you're on your way. Go get him so we can save him."

"Uncle Harry, Bill," I said to the two men. "Petra knows what to do with the Chief's body. Take care of it while I fetch Jason."

I strode out of the house to the sounds of the rest of them hustling to attend to their errands. It felt wrong for a moment, the fact that I had people, humans no less, listening to me and following my requests but as we were all fighting for the same result, I guess it didn't matter.

I threw myself into the air and within a minute, I was landing on the front step of Jason's parents' house. The door opened and a woman who looked remarkably like the DCI opened the door.

"Alexander? He's upstairs in bed. What's wrong with him?"

"Eirwen is dead," I cut to the chase. "His mind is imploding and unless we do something now, he will die."

"Nothing like straight talking," a tall man from the top of the stair stated, a hint of a chuckle within the concern of his voice. "I'm Frankie, Jason's father. Vanessa said you can help."

"Well, I can't, but Y'cart can. Do you know where she lives?"

They nodded the affirmative. I directed them to start the fifteen minute drive, around the roadworks and one way streets that made Blackpool a rat trap at times. I walked into Jason's bedroom and almost buckled at the power of the agony that the boy was in. I leaned over his bed, pulling the covers back to pick him up but as my hands touched his body, the overwhelming crushing power of death clawed at my own mind.

I gritted my teeth, promising myself once more that I would never put a human through the bonding process and gently wrapped the lad in a blanket. This lessened the contact between us and I found that I could easily lift him and carry him through the house and out onto the street. With a quick word, I glimmered to make sure no-one saw me with Jason and lifted myself into the air.

With Jason safely tucked up in a spare room at Y'cart's, his mind asleep from the potion, I turned to the rest. Vanessa's complexion was drawn and pale as she talked quietly to her family, while Petra and Bill cleaned themselves having disposed of the Chief's body.

"Why don't we call it a night and start up again tomorrow?" I suggested. "I think that we are all out on our feet here."

"I have still got to look at your uncle's wound," Y'cart argued. "But there is no reason why the rest can't go and get some sleep."

"We're going to have a little wander around town first, then head back," Petra said. "We'll meet back here at dusk?"

I watched them leave, Vanessa deciding to go with her sister while Bill and Petra nodded a brief farewell to me. Y'cart was fussing over Uncle Harry, pulling his shirt up, exposing three nasty claw marks on his side. Blood was still weeping slightly from them, a tribute to the sharpness of the werewolf claws.

"Um, does this mean that I am going to turn into one?" Harry asked, concern in his voice.

"Relax Harry," Y'cart soothed. "Only a bite from an Alpha can turn you, not just a scratch like this."

"This is a scratch?" his voice crept up an octave as the witch applied a foul smelling salve.

"I've had worse," I remarked, causing Harry to glance over.

"But you've got your own healing abilities," he winced as Y'cart began to bandage up his side. He sat down gingerly at the table, taking a glass of a purple liquid from Y'cart. He raised it to his nose, which turned up as he took in the odour. I took the offered cup of coffee, sipping at it to savour the taste. I glanced out of the kitchen window, noting that we still had a couple of hours before sunrise. The kitchen clock showed that it was a little after six in the morning which confirmed my timings.

"So are we any closer to finding out who they are?" Y'cart asked as she took a seat by the side of Harry. "Other than the dead policeman, I mean."

"I'm erring back to the Norris's," I said regretfully. "CS Leighton went bonkers when Detective Jackson suggested that they were involved and there was this weird thing that he said when he was with the Alpha."

"What thing?" they both asked simultaneously.

"Before he turned, he told the Alpha that he had brought me for the easy kill and it looked like the Alpha was upset," I frowned. "Then he said that he hadn't been told to leave me alone."

"So you think that the Alpha knows you and protecting you?" Harry queried.

"That and the damn wolf bit me," I rubbed my arm at the memory of the pain. "It just sat there, watching me, waiting for me to turn."

"So you think that rather than killing you, he wanted to bring you into the pack," Y'cart stated, rather than asked. I nodded.

"Looks like we may have to pay them a visit in the morning then," Harry yawned as his body reacted to the healing salve that Y'cart had applied. I could already see his eyes drooping closed and I scooted around to support his body before he fell from his chair.

"I think he better stay here tonight," Y'cart suggested. "I've got a third bedroom upstairs so he will be fine."

I half smiled to myself as I carried Harry upstairs, putting him on the bed that Y'cart had indicated. Walking back down into the kitchen, I saw her wiping her eyes and my heart softened towards her. Forgoing my usual distaste of witches, I walked up and gave her a hug.

"We will get them and kill them," I told her. "They will pay for killing Eirwen, I promise you that."

"Just be careful, Alexander," she laid her head on the top of mine. "Eirwen made me promise that if anything happened to her, I was to take care of you, not that you need taking care of." She added quickly as I bristled in her arms.

"What was she doing in America?" I asked suddenly.

"What do you mean?"

"When I first got here, Eirwen was in the USA and off the grid. What was she doing?"

"I assume it was when she was tracking down information about Beddows' plan to bring his sister back from the dead," Y'cart replied. "But now I'm not so sure."

"Why not? I guess it kind of makes sense as there are Council members who live the other side of the Atlantic."

"She was planning on going back next month. She said that she was tracking something down but wouldn't say what."

"Well, I guess we'll never know, unless she comes back as a ghost," I sighed. "Knowing my luck, I'll get haunted by the damn lycans."

I broke the hug and finished off my cup of coffee. I could see that Y'cart was stifling a yawn.

"I'm going to go out and have a quick look around before heading back home." I flashed her a knowing smile. "Go and be with Harry." I didn't give her a chance to reply as I blurred from the room, out into the street and found a warm air current to ride high in the sky.

I always found it calming to let myself float at several hundred metres up. Far enough away from the ground that you didn't hear the hustle and bustle but not too high to risk getting caught up in the stronger airflows that whipped around the planet. Centuries before, I had found out the hard way, the painful way, about losing control of myself in flight. An argument with a cliff face, which I lost, is not the most productive way to spend an evening; waiting for your bones to heal while waves washed over you lying on the rocks.

I circled the town centre, my eyes observing the few all night revellers and night shift workers that were on their way home, or the early risers getting ready for another day at work. I thought about what Eirwen's death would mean to me. Yes she had been my mother figures for six and a half centuries and I had loved her dearly and knew that she loved me like the son that she never had the opportunity to bear, but we had not seen each other in over a hundred years until a couple of months ago. I had to admit to being partly jealous, partly angry and partly happy for her when I found out how she had been living for the last seventy years while I had been a vagrant, eeking out a life wherever I could.

But now she was gone. All that was left of her was the memory in my heart of the woman who had saved my life and I vowed to myself, to her and to the very Prince of Darkness himself, that I would avenge her death.

My musings were interrupted with a surprising jolt of recognition as I looked along the sea front promenade. My eyes were immediately drawn to the blonde hair of Petra, skulking in the shadows as she tracked someone down the street. I looked around and couldn't see Bill so, with a tinge of concern for her that made me wonder why I felt it, I landed on quiet feet on the rooftop of the shops. I crept along, easily keeping up, jumping the short distances between the buildings until my vision narrowed in on her prey.

It was a small framed lad with short brown hair who had his hands buried deep in the pockets of his winter coat as he battled against the bitter wind that howled along the road. Litter cycloned up around the pedestrians but Petra and the boy both ignored it, both intent on their own missions. The boy caught his foot on a crooked paving stone, stumbling slightly and I caught a glimpse of his face. Seeing the determination in Petra's eyes, I quickly jumped off the roof, glimmer intact and I made my way in front of him before allowing my glyph to ease away.

"Alex? What are you doing here?" the boy asked as he took four quick steps up to me.

"Oh, hey Jake, I couldn't sleep so thought I'd have a walk. What about you?"

"I, um, I woke up and my parents had already left for the factory," he stammered. "Sarah-Louise wasn't in either which was strange but then I got a text from her saying to meet her near the arcade."

"Well, let's go and meet her then," I smiled at him. "She shouldn't be walking around on her own."

I could feel the frustration pouring out of Petra as I clapped my friend on the shoulder. Despite what I had said earlier, I still had serious reservations that Jake was a lycan. There was too much that just didn't add up for him to be one. We traded bad jokes as we walked the short distance to the arcade and my stomach flipped as my gaze fell on the long, dark brown hair of his sister. A flash of memory tingled through my mind and I realised why I had subconsciously been dreaming of my Lady Catherine recently as Sarah-Louise bore a striking resemblance to my long lost first love.

Jake broke from my side, running over to his sister, hugging her and muttering out how scared he had been to wake up alone in their house. I saw her chocolate brown eyes wince as he embraced her and, as they left her brother to meet my own eyes, I saw pain mixed with another confused emotion in her expression.

"Alex, what are you doing out at this time of night?" she asked. "Shouldn't you be in bed?"

"Shouldn't you?" I joked. "I mean, won't both your parents and my uncle have a fit if they find out?"

"I always go for a walk in the morning when I wake up," Jake offered. "It clears my head sometimes."

"From what?" I asked.

"I kind of get these weird dreams sometimes," he replied, his forehead crinkling with worry.

"He watches too many horror films," Sarah-Louise rubbed the top of his head. "I tell him not to, Mum tells him not to, even Dad tells him not to watch them but he does anyway."

"So why are you out this early?" I asked, trying to take the attention away from the now blushing Jake.

"I was round a friend's house and we had a bit of a argument," she shrugged. I saw her wince again. "I think I've hurt my arm."

"Let me see," Jake insisted. He turned to me. "I did my First Aiders badge, remember?"

I watched as he undid his sister's coat, not having noticed that she only had one arm through and even I had to wince as I saw bone poking through the skin. It looked like she'd had more than an argument.

"Jeez sis, you need to go to the hospital," Jake moaned. "I can't do anything about that."

"Doesn't it hurt," I queried, noting the lack of true pain from her. It was almost like she was making a show of the pain for our benefit.

"I took some pain killers before I left," she flashed a look at me. "Your face looks a lot better."

"My face?" I asked. Jake looked at me.

"Yeah Alex, all of your bruises have gone from the fight with those lads at the arcade," my friend said, reaching out to touch my face. I cursed to myself, not realising when I unleashed my healing abilities earlier in the evening from the knocks I received while fighting the lycans that they would have healed all of my injuries.

"Look, why don't we get you to the hospital?" I suggested to Sarah-Louise, trying to divert their attention back to her injured arm.

"Jake, will you go and get me a bottle of water so that I can pop another pain killer?" she asked her brother and as he turned to jog to the nearest shop, she leaned in to me as we walked slowly along the road.

"You've only got twenty minutes until sunrise so you'd better go and hide yourself away."

"What.. what do you mean?" I stuttered.

"Unless you want to flame up, you need to get yourself inside," she smiled at me.

"I don't know what you think you know," I started but she raised a finger and touched it to my lips.

"It's such as shame because I think you're a really cute guy," she sighed. "I was hoping that I could get you to join us, to become my mate but you showed me that I made a mistake with my choice when you shook off the effects of my bite."

I stopped dead, my eyes boring into her. She had a sad smile on her face as she turned to look back at me. My mind was racing and I felt my nails automatically lengthening as my self-defence skills took over.

"You haven't got time to kill me now and in front of all of these people," she paused. "Even a vampire wouldn't break the rules, would you?"

"You are a lycan," I stated flatly, before her earlier statement filtered into my brain. "You're the Alpha?"

"Life's a bitch, Alex, and so am I," she chuckled. "I need to replace a pack member now that you and that human bitch killed Greg so I'm going to have to speed up my brother's conversion."

"Jake isn't one? I thought that you kept everything in the family, so why the Chief?"

"Greg is, ah, was my Mum's step-brother and too good a detective for his own good. But when he found out what we could offer him, he jumped at the chance of being converted and hid the Varseys' bones."

"Why did you kill them?"

"That family cast a slur against mine which I couldn't allow to continue," she shrugged. "I don't take rejection well, so Vinny really shouldn't have dumped me for that little bitch that he started dating."

"You killed them because a boy dumped you?" I gasped.

"Vampires do worse, don't you? Even lycans joined with your kind to get rid of that van Hightinger weirdo at the beginning of the last century."

"Brynhild," I huffed. "So what now?"

"I'd suggest that you move to another place and leave my range to my pack… but somehow I doubt you're going to do that are you?"

"You killed Eirwen and I made a promise that I would avenge her. I will kill you and your pack." I took a step back as I saw Jake finally reappearing from the shop. I frowned. "Do us both a favour. Don't turn your brother. I like him. I'd hate to have to kill him as well."

"You're just a single, lone vampire," Sarah-Louise laughed at me. "Who do you think that you are to think that you can threaten my pack?"

"My name is Alexander of Farrow's Haven. My teacher was Paulinos de Balurac, slayer of the lycan Kiran Gestarde," I paused as I felt fear shiver through her body at the name of the vicious Alpha Prime lycan. "My sire is Chlothar Pfaff and I was his most trusted. I wield Venenum Draconum, the Bane of Dragons and I will protect the people of this range from your kind."

"Well then, Alexander," she huffed. "We will see you in the woods."

I cast a glance at Jake who had become distracted by a large stuffed wolf toy that had fallen from a stand outside an arcade so I cast myself into the air, catching a current and within minutes was landing in the communal gardens of Harry's housing block, just as the sun's rays brightened the sky.

Michael Andrews

Chapter Thirteen

Screams echoed around the castle. Night had come quickly and we thought that we were ready for them but as the moon's rays shone down onto the courtyard, I could hear Captain Paulinos swearing at the number of lycans that had breached the walls. We had expected the attack, coming just one lunar cycle after the Captain had killed Kiran Gestarde, the lycan Alpha Prime, but Chlothar had never envisaged that the beasts would be able to co-ordinate an attack in such large numbers.

I could see serfs running for their lives, trying to avoid the claws and fangs of the wolf pack and my mind ached to jump from the balcony into the fray to defend our people. A steadying hand on my shoulder made me stand my ground.

"Not yet, my Alexander," Chlothar's deep voice instructed me. "Let the warriors do their work."

"But sire, my job is to protect the castle and those within," I argued.

"Your job is to protect our Sire," Captain Paulinos snapped at me, before leaping into the fray. I growled at the thought of being kept out of the fight but as I saw Eirwen fly into battle alongside our other warriors, I contented myself with watching the fight unfold.

"Watch carefully, my young servant," Chlothar said. "Watch how your mother and the Captain engage the lycan scum and learn how best to slaughter them."

As the fight continued, it was clear that the wolves did not have the co-ordination or strategic fighting skills that we vampires possessed. This was no hunt, which they were used to, but a revenge attack and it became clear that they had relied on their superior numbers for their advantage.

When our warriors began to scythe through their ranks, they soon became disorganised, degenerating into individuals fighting their own survival battles. Chlothar and I stood watching, observing the fall of the lycan pack with a sense of satisfaction. That was until a lone wolf managed to scale the wall and land on the balcony. It snarled at the pair of us and leapt. Without hesitation, I jumped in front of Chlothar, his protection at the forefront of my mind. I raised my arms and swiped them in a crisscross pattern in front of my body, my claws sinking deep into the flesh of the animal. I sank my teeth into its throat, my razor sharp incisors easily penetrating the flesh and I felt the beast panic as it realised that I was not simply a boy standing with his father.

I gripped the wolf's fur, holding it tightly, not allowing it to escape as its blood flowed into my mouth. It was the first time that I had ever drunk the blood of another paranormal creature and the kick that it was giving me was far stronger than that of a human victim. I felt the wolf's struggles weaken and finally Chlothar put his hand on my neck.

"That is enough, Alexander," he told me. "The beast will die and you need to stop feeding."

"But Sire, the feeling... I can't describe it." My body felt stronger than it had ever felt. I knew that I could take on the world and survive if my master desired me to.

"You did well, Alexander as did our warriors," Chlothar smiled. "The battle is not yet over. You did your job.

Now it is time to clean the vermin from my House. Attend my side and fight hard."

He jumped over the side of the balcony and I scrambled to join him. As I landed by his side, a wolf attacked. I brought up my fist, smashing it into the jaw of the beast. The wolf howled in pain, slumping on the ground as Chlothar unsheathed his sword and buried it deep in the chest of the now limp animal. Sounds of pain, both human and lupine echoed around the courtyard as we moved onto the next target.

I sat up and looked around. My bed sheet was shredded, a testament to the sharpness of my claws and I winced as I saw a long, deep wound in my arm. The drapes around the bed were still drawn tight and I sat for a moment, thinking about my latest dream. Lycans had evolved in the seven hundred years since that attack on our castle and I prayed that I would be strong enough to cope with this latest encounter. My heart ached as I thought of Eirwen's dead body, lying in a bed at Y'cart's house when the empty feeling within the house reminded me that Harry had also stayed at the witch's. However, I could feel a presence downstairs so with quiet feet, I slipped from the room, my vision switching over to hunting mode, my claws extending slightly ready to attack if the intruder proved to be an enemy. As I edged into the kitchen, I saw a faint glow coming from the room. A chill swept over the room as I stepped in, my hands hanging by my side.

"My dearest Alexander," the sweet voice echoed.
"Eirwen?" I stuttered at the ghostly image of my former mother.
"My time is short, my dearest one, so heed my words well. There is a presence behind the lycan pack, one whom may look to attack. Hide thee well and be thee

meek, for your presence is one they seek. If they discover you here, then attack without fear, for if you are subdued, then your servitude will be renewed."

"What do you mean?" I asked. However, the image was already fading and I was overwhelmed with feelings of worry, of fear, and finally of relief. Then, I no longer felt her and in my heart I knew that Eirwen had finally passed over to whatever lies beyond death, in the realm that not even the mightiest necromancers can penetrate.

"Alex? Are you okay?" Petra's voice startled me out of my thoughts.

"Jeez Petra! Don't creep up on me like that," I pulled my claws back into my fingers.

"Who were you talking to?" she asked, her eyes searching the room.

"You wouldn't believe me if I told you," I mumbled under my breath before telling her 'just myself.'

"What's wrong with your arm?" Bill stepped into the room, his eyes a mystery.

"I think I cut myself while having another dream this afternoon," I sighed. "But the dream did remind me how to divide and fight the lycans. I also want my sword with me this time."

"But I thought that only silver weapons would kill a lycan," Petra questioned. "Or a vampire bleeding them dry of course."

"My sword isn't a normal sword," I explained. "It has enough magic within its making to kill any paranormal being. Trust me, it works on lycans." I grinned viciously at the thought of getting revenge on Eirwen's killers.

"So we were following that Jake kid this morning when you jumped in," the blonde huntress huffed. "I was about to corner him when you interrupted me."

"Jake isn't a lycan," I argued. "At least not yet he isn't."

"How do you know?" Bill interrupted Petra's retort.

"Because the Alpha told me," I sighed. Both hunters eyebrows shot up and I had to refrain from giggling at the comedic effect. "Sarah-Louise Norris is the Alpha. Jake doesn't know a thing about them, yet."

"How are you sure?"

"She told him," Bill sighed. "I saw the look of regret in her eyes when she was talking to Alex."

"Regret?" Harry asked as he walked into the kitchen, dashing any hope that I had of keeping him away from the fight that I knew was coming this evening.

"I think that she kind of likes me," I shrugged. "She wanted me in her pack, and I think not just as an ordinary pack member."

"What makes you think that?" he asked.

"Didn't you see the eyes that she was making at him at the party for the Chief?" DCI Bach asked as she followed Uncle Harry in. I sighed as another human was going to be put at risk.

"She told me the reason why the Varseys were killed," I started. "It turns out that Vincent Varsey was dating her before he broke off their relationship for another girl."

"So she killed the whole family in revenge?" Petra gasped. "What a bitch."

"That's a lycan for you," I shrugged.

"Well where did the Chief come into it?" the DCI asked as she stretched, loosening up her upper torso.

"He was Helen Norris's step brother," Harry replied for me, causing me to look in his direction. "Hey, I'm a detective. It's what I do. Investigate things."

"Well, Sarah-Louise knows what I am and her pack is going to be waiting for me at the nature reserve," I said. I braced myself. "I'm going alone."

"Like hell you are," Harry stated.

"Don't be stupid," the DCI argued.

"This is our job as well, Alex," Petra sighed. "Look Alex, I'm getting to know how you think."

"Really? You, a sixteen year old human hunter knows how a millennia old vampire thinks?"

"No, but I know how the vampire who's decided to care about humans thinks," she shrugged. "You want to try to keep us all out of harm's way but by doing so, you will end up getting yourself killed. Like it or not, we're going to help."

I looked at the four of them, seeing steely determination in their eyes. I knew that I wasn't going to win this one, just like the last time when we went up against Beddows van Hightinger and his vampire pack. That day, we lost someone. We had already lost Eirwen to the lycans and I wasn't going to lose anyone else.

"Okay, fine. Bill, Petra, you must have silver weapons in your armoury," I half asked. "Make sure that Uncle Harry and Vanessa have them as anything else is not going to protect them." I watched as Bill turned to go back to his house next door, before turning back to Harry. "Where's Y'cart?"

"She's going to stay behind to look after Jason," he replied. "She said that there isn't a great deal that she can do against werewolves so we thought it best for her to keep out of it."

"Makes sense Alex," Vanessa added. "She's also our best healer so when this is over, she can patch up any injuries without us having to explain to a hospital."

While Bill was equipping the others with silver bullets and knives, I took the opportunity to get myself dressed in my usual black t-shirt, black hoodie and black tracksuit bottoms. I strapped Venenum Draconum to my side and picked up a holster of shuriken. While I knew that they wouldn't kill a werewolf, they certainly hurt and would slow down any attacker. As I headed back out onto the landing, I paused at the door leading into Connor's bedroom. It was slightly ajar, which was unusual and I pushed it open.

The room looked as it always did. Nothing was out of place. Apart from it being far too neat and tidy for a teenage boy's room, it looked as though it was just waiting for Connor to reappear. A sudden chill came over me and for a moment, I thought I saw something at the window but having covered the distance in a split second, all I could see was the shadows of the communal gardens.

Shaking off the feeling, I headed back downstairs to find everyone else standing in the lounge, waiting to go. I nodded to Bill and, as he lead the way into the gardens, my eyes persistently scanning the area, looking for signs of something, anything out of place. I saw nothing so I turned to the four humans.

"You guys go on ahead in the cars," I started. "I'll take to wing and scout from above."

"Good idea, Alex," Bill agreed. "Is there any way you can message us if you see something?"

"He could shout?" Petra giggled. "He's very good at shouting at me."

I flashed her a grin before pulling out the phone that Harry had gotten me and waved it at them. I watched them enter the elevator and as soon as the door closed, I leapt into the air, climbing to a suitable height where I could watch the blocks around them.

I needn't have bothered with my plan though as we arrived at Marton Mere without incident. I landed next to Harry's car just as they were getting out. Each of them were patting each other down, checking that they had their weapons secured on their bodies and I turned to Harry.

"Look Harry. I know it's pointless asking you to stay out of this, so I just want to ask you to be careful," I started. "You've seen what one wolf can do. This will be the full pack."

"But if there is three of them, then you need back up," he argued. "And you're right. It is pointless asking me to stand by while you go out and risk your neck… again!"

I let him pull me into a hug, knowing that he missed Connor and a flash of guilt ran through me for not telling him that Connor wasn't dead. Well, not properly dead anyway. When he let me go, he ruffled my hair, causing me to scowl at him.

"Connor hated me doing that as well," he chuckled. "Come on, let's go kill some werewolves."

"I bet three months ago you would never have dreamed of saying that," Vanessa smiled. "It's amazing how quickly you adapt to the real world once your eyes have been opened."

"I still can't get over how many myths are actually real," Harry scratched his head. "I mean, Alex will be telling me that dragons and unicorns exist next."

"Don't be stupid," I replied as I finished tying my left trainer that had come lose during my flight. "Unicorns were made up by bad troubadours in the Twelfth Century and dragons died out centuries ago."

I looked up at the sudden silence. All four of them were stood, mouths open, staring at me.

"What?" I asked.

"Dragons existed?" Petra asked.

"Of course they did. Mean spirited bleeders though. I was glad to hear that the last couple were killed off."

"You're pulling our legs," Harry insisted. "Come on, let's get going."

We turned to head into the trees. I took the lead, Harry and Vanessa following me with the two hunters bringing up the rear.

Chapter Fourteen

The silence in the woods was deafening. It seemed that Mother Nature knew of the unnatural confrontation that was coming and had pulled a vanishing act, hiding all of her creatures and animals out of harm's way. Not even the hoot of an owl or the scurrying of a field mouse could mask the tread of my four companions as we made our way through the undergrowth.

I had warned the others not to be shocked by my appearance when they saw me from the front and had given myself over to a full vampire conversion. I could already pick up the sounds of my companions breathing, my vision etched with faint heat signatures as I scanned the trees, looking for any sign of the three remaining lycans.

We had decided to start by looking at the clearing where Chief Leighton had brought me to die but other than the small traces of blood that remained, there was no sign of the lycans.

"Should we split up?" Bill asked. "We'll cover more ground that way."

"I think we should stick together," Harry responded. "From what Alex told us, they are going to be waiting for us anyway so we need to be as large a group as possible to attack them."

"I agree with Harry, Uncle Bill," Petra nodded. "Lycans prefer to pick off individuals rather than attack as a whole.

The Comitia had records of a massive offence by lycans in the Fourteenth Century against one of the vampire Houses and they were wiped out, almost to a wolf."

"Really?" Bill asked. "Is that something you know about Alex?"

I couldn't help but grin viciously at the memory of my dream, and of the past. I knew that my incisors were showing but hey, they wanted to run around with a vampire.

"I should do," I smiled. "I was there. It was my first fight against lycans. It was fun."

"You turning savage on us?" Vanessa poked me. I shook my head before continuing on the path.

"As much as the movies like to portray werewolves as pack animals, the reality is that anything more than half a dozen members will break the pack as the stronger wolves battle out for the Alpha or Beta positions," I explained. "The pack fragments into factions and they lose the ability to co-ordinate. However, Sarah-Louise only has her parents left in her pack so expect them to be in sync with each other."

"If we kill her, will the others change back?" Harry asked.

"Doubtful," I replied. "I think that if they were newly converted then there could be a chance but by the sound of it, they have been a family pack for a while."

"What about Jake?"

"Jake isn't a worry, he won't be here," I insisted. "I think I'll have a quick scout to see if I can draw them out."

"Wait..." Petra started but I was already airborne.

However, being so close to so many trees wasn't conducive to low level flying so I landed on the branches of the nearest tree before jumping from tree to tree. I felt like a monkey, or a kid at the playground, but as I made my way through the woods, I was growing frustrated at the lack of sight or sound of the lycan pack. I made my way back to the others, startling Petra as I landed just in front of them.

"Jesus Alex, I could have taken your head off!" she swore at me as she pulled the swing of her dirk.

"You wish," I muttered under my breath. I noticed that she gave me a funny look before I turned to the rest of them. "I'm confused. I've been all over the woods and I cannot get even a sniff that they are here and trust me… I can smell a lycan."

"So where are they then?" Harry asked, just as his phone bleeped. He cursed several times having paled into whiteness. "It's Sammy Jackson. He says that there are reports of wild animals terrorising punters on the Pleasure Beach."

"What?" I gasped. "It can't be them. An Alpha should know better than to expose their kind to humans."

"Only one way to find out if it's them," Bill huffed as he shouldered his rifle. "I guess we're off to the front."

"You go on ahead, Alex," Vanessa suggested. "Be careful but save as many people as you can."

"Sammy says that there is a kid trapped on the rails of The Big One. Here's a photo he's sent." Harry added. I took the phone and looked at the picture.

"That's Jake," I swore.

"It's got to be a trap," Petra warned. "They're using your friendship to lure you in."

"That might be so, but I've still got to go after him."

"Be careful and we'll get there as soon as we can," Harry told me.

I looked at them and nodded before throwing myself into the air. As I sped over the rooftops, my glimmer glyph intact, I wondered why the hell Sarah-Louise would break rules that had been laid down millennia before. By attacking humans in a public setting she was risking, no she was encouraging, all sides in the paranormal world to exterminate her pack. The general human populace just isn't equipped to deal with the fact that there are beings like us in existence.

I landed on the rooftop of Edna's café. Normally I liked using this as a landing spot as Edna dealt out a mean coffee but tonight my mind was focused on the problem in hand. I looked out onto the Pleasure Beach, hearing the screams of adults and small children alike. I ground my teeth in anger at the thought that kids were being indiscriminately targeted and quickly scaled down the drainpipe and ran towards the nearest entrance to the fun park, changing back into human mode as soon as I touched the ground.

"Here now kid," a uniformed policeman tried to grab me. "There's been a break out from the zoo so you can't go in there."

"But sir, my little brother is in there," I pleaded, putting on my best puppy dog eyes.

"There are wild animals in there kid," he insisted. "I can't let you go in."

I'd had enough of wasting time and while I knew that I could incapacitate him in an instant, he was just doing his job. I looked him in the eye once more, fixing his gaze to mine. Pushing my mind onto his, I overpowered his thoughts with my hypnovision and, while I couldn't force him to allow me through as that was going too far against his beliefs, I did persuade him to turn around to look out at the sea while I slipped past him.

I rubbed my temples to ease the pressure that always builds up when vampires use their hypnotic powers on humans, and I saw people running in every direction. Why do humans always run around like idiots when they panic?

I heard a low growl to my left and spun around, my claws instinctively lengthening in defence.

"Shit!" I was face to face with a lion. It was a young female, creeping on slow paws towards me. I tried to touch her mind, to allow my empathic senses touch hers but she was too far gone in the hunt. I could hear screams, echoing around the rides which were, for once, not the cause of the yells. The young lioness leapt at me and I dodged to the side. Any hope that I had that she would give up as she went skidding past me were short lived as, with an angry roar, she turned and charged once more. Cursing in frustration, I grabbed hold of the animal, wrapping my arms around it, positioning myself so that I was out of reach of her teeth, I gently but firmly squeezed her neck, cutting off the flow of air from her lungs.

I felt the struggle of the lioness as she turned from hunter to prey but I had no intention of killing her. After all, she was only doing what came naturally to her. It wasn't her fault that she had somehow gotten free. I held on tightly until I felt the body go limp and I left her sleeping on the ground. I looked around to see several other lions tracking various pleasure seekers but despite the sounds of wolves, I couldn't see any.

"ALEX!!" I heard a young boy's shout. "HELP! Please help me."

"Jake?" I looked in the direction of his voice and saw my new friend, cowering, clinging to the rail of The Big One while a fully grown male tiger was pawing at the air as it leapt, missing him by mere inches. I could feel the fear flowing from him, definitely not something that a full blown lycan would be experiencing so I leapt into the air, catching the tiger in mid-jump, smashing it to the ground. I passed over into vamp mode, strengthening my body as the tiger turned and charged.

Despite living in captivity for most of its life, the tiger was still born with natural hunting instincts and we circled each other, my objective keeping it away from the sobbing Jake. I heard Jake shout a warning and turned in his direction just as a second tiger attacked. I cursed to myself, remembering the lessons that I had been taught about animal predators hunting in pairs and howled in pain as I felt long teeth sink into my thigh.

Snarling, I sliced downwards, racking the tiger's throat with my claws. It yowled as it released me, staggering away in pain. The original tiger took the opportunity to attack but I'd had enough of playing nice with the animals. My sword flashed and easily carved through flesh as I caught the leap of the tiger, slicing it in two. The animal twitched for a few moments as its death slowly registered in its brain and I turned back to see Jake staring at me, wide eyed.

"You are a frigging vampire!" he hissed at me. "I didn't believe her but it's true, isn't it?"

"You didn't believe who?" I asked, fighting to turn myself back. However, the adrenaline was pumping through my veins and I could almost taste the blood that had been spilled. I looked at Jake and shook my head to clear it. I could almost feel the primal instinct inside me but, counting to five, I calmed myself down. When I opened my eyes, I was looking through normal eyes once more.

"Sarah-Louise. She said you were a vampire and couldn't be trusted," Jake clung to the rollercoaster rail.

"Look, let's talk about that in a second but we need to get you down from there," I told him. "Jump and I'll catch you."

"Sod off!" he sobbed. "You'll eat me or something."

"Jake, mate, you're my buddy," I insisted. "If I was going to eat you, I'd have done it before now. I've had plenty of chances but I haven't, have I?"

"No… I guess not," he replied. He looked at me and at the sword that I still had in my hand. "Why does a vampire need a sword anyway?"

"To stop hungry tigers from eating their friends," I chuckled, which brought a small smile back to his face. "Look Jake, seriously, I just want to make sure that you're safe. Come on, drop down and I'll catch you."

I watched as he nodded and squirmed around on the rail before twisting his body so that he was hanging off. He swore.

"What's wrong?" I asked.
"I've snagged my top. I'm stuck."
"Hold on."

I jumped, easily clearing the fifteen foot height difference to land on the rail beside him. He looked at me wide eyed as I unfastened his jacket that had become trapped in between the rail and the metal frame. I offered him my back and with him securely wrapping his arms around my neck, I eased myself off the frame and lowered myself to the ground.

"That was so cool!" he giggled. "So you really are a vampire?"

"Yeah, but keep it quiet," I said, before putting on a mock horror voice. "Or I'll have to eat you, little boy!"

"Shut up!" he pushed me away. I turned serious.

"How did you get up there?"

"Um, my sister put me up there. She said that it was to protect me from the animals."

"How did she get you up there?"

"She's like mega strong. It's funny cos her arm is all healed up today as well. Is she a vampire as well?"

"No, she isn't. She's something worse." I said it before I was able to stop myself. After all, Sarah-Louise is his sister.

"What do you mean?"

"Jake, I'm sorry to be the one to tell you but your family are lycans. Werewolves," I added as a confused look spread across his face.

"I knew that something was up with them," he mumbled. "It's why we keep moving, isn't it. They kill people."

"Yeah buddy. Do you know where they are? If I don't find them, they are going to kill some other people tonight."

"I'm not sure but something my sister said makes sense now," he frowned. "She said that if I see a blood sucking moron, then I was to tell him that he shouldn't get so easily distracted. What does that mean?"

A chill ran through me. Distractions. Had I fallen for the easiest and simplest ploy to divide and conquer your opponents?

"It means that she's tricked me. She deliberately put you in danger to get me away from my friends."

"Bitch," he swore. "She kept on at me about being friends with you and trying to get you to come over."

"She wanted me in her pack. She even bit me last night to try to turn me,"

"Are you the one who hurt her?"

"No, that was my mother, well, step-mother. Sarah-Louise and your Uncle Greg killed her."

"I'm sorry," a tear ran down his cheek. "Am I a werewolf too?"

"No," I told him in a confident voice. "She has to bring you over into the pack so unless she's bitten you, which I'm guessing not, then you're still human."

"Good. I don't want to be a werewolf." I saw a sudden dawning of comprehension spread across his face. "Did she, did they, um did my family kill Adrian Varsey and his family? We were on holiday together and then they went without saying goodbye."

"I, ah," I paused.

"Adrian was my best mate and he hasn't emailed me, text me, Facebooked me or called me back." I saw tears welling in his eyes.

"Yeah, I'm afraid so," I hugged him to me as he cried for his friend. "Sarah-Louise said that it was because Vincent dumped her."

"Cos she was being a bitch to him," he huffed.

"I need to go, Jake," I said softly. "My friends are in trouble. Go to that man over there and he will look after you." I pointed at Detective Jackson who was scanning the Pleasure Beach. "Tell him that Harry Shepherd's nephew sent you and that they only need to tranquilize the animals here."

"Where will you be?" Jake asked.

"I'm going to stop your family from killing mine."

"Good luck Alex, and Alex… don't let them kill anyone else."

I pulled him into a hug and he whispered into my ear. My body stiffened at his words before he let me go and turned to run towards Sammy Jackson. With a steely determination now set in my body, I cast my glimmer glyph and jumped skywards to fly back to the nature reserve as fast as I could.

Michael Andrews

Chapter Fifteen

I didn't need any of my vampire senses to locate the others as I reached Marton Mere once again. There was enough noise to wake the dead, literally, and as I sped overhead to Harry's location, my eyes boggled at what I saw.

Where I had expected just Sarah-Louise and her parents to be attacking, there were werewolves by the dozen. I saw DCI Bach being hard pressed by two wolves as she backed herself into a narrow gap between two rocks and I landed on the back of the nearest, flattening it to the ground as my momentum broke the beast's back. It howled in pain before I silenced it with my sword, slicing through the neck, sending its head rolling down the slight incline on the ground.

"Alex! You're back!" she gasped as she was clawed by her attacked. She looked down at her torn shirt, a frown spreading across her face. "You did not just ruin this shirt!" she hissed and she stabbed forwards with the long knife that she was wielding. I heard the pop of gooey matter as the point of the knife pierced the eyeball of the wolf and the DCI pushed with all of her weight until the blade was embedded firmly into the brain. The beast collapsed onto the floor, twitching in its death throes until Vanessa pulled the knife out. I grimaced as she wiped the grey brain cells from the blade onto her shirt and she looked at me with a cocked head.

"Well it's ruined now anyway," she shrugged before pulling a gun from her belt and firing over my shoulder. I rubbed my now deafened ear as I turned to see another body on the ground, its paws outstretched towards me.

"There's too many wolves here," I cursed at her.

"Tell us about it," she snapped back. "What happened to 'there's only three' and 'they don't play well in packs?'"

"They don't!" I insisted and cut down another wolf as it launched itself at us. "Let's get to the others."

We began a slow, battled walk, edging out of the corner that the DCI had taken refuge in, stabbing and slicing our way through wolf attack after wolf attack. I was seriously concerned for the others, especially Harry as he'd had no training, but as we rounded the edge of the trees, I saw the three of them back to back in a classic outnumbered fighters pose.

Petra had slung her crossbow and opted for her dirks, both hands a blur as she fought to keep the pack of wolves at bay. Bill showed his years of swordsmanship with a dazzling display of hand control while Harry alternated between the dirk that he had borrowed from Petra and his gun, firing silver bullets whenever he could.

I jumped into the fray, no longer willing to expose my friends to the dangers that they faced. I caught a wolf as it leapt at Petra, my fangs barred, biting into the jugular of the beast. I tore my mouth away, ripping flesh and veins alike, dumping the animal on the ground as more lycans spilled into the clearing.

"Where are they all coming from?" Bill yelled.

"I haven't got a clue," I shouted back as I ducked a clawed swipe that would have taken my head from my shoulders. I thrust forwards with my sword, catching the wolf in the ribs and twisted, spilling its guts onto the mossy carpet of grass.

"It's like every werewolf has come out to get us," Petra cursed as she stabbed her attacker through the eye in a similar fashion to the DCI moments earlier.

"There has to be a reason for it," Harry gasped as his wolf reopened the wound from the night before. He pulled his gun and shot the lycan in the head, giving a satisfied grunt as the beast stopped dead and fell where it stood.

A loud howl echoed in the clearing and suddenly, the attack stopped. The five of us stood, weapons drawn, the four humans panting in various states of exhaustion. Bodies littered the clearing, each lycan having returned to human form upon its death.

Humans of all shapes and sizes lay around us but, thankfully, none of them looked to be a kid. I saw Ian Norris's body just off to the side of Harry, half of his face missing from where my Uncle's bullet had torn into the lycan's head.

"What's happening?" Petra asked as she took the reprieve to pick up her crossbow and load in six bolts. I was impressed at the modification that she had made, allowing it to become a multiple loading weapon, rather than the single shot bow of old.

"I'm not sure," I replied as I edged my way around the four humans.

I saw movement from the corner of my eye and I saw the lycans drop to their haunches as Sarah-Louise walked into the clearing. She was wearing a loose fitting, body length tunic and the way that she strode showed the confidence of an Alpha. Walking beside her was a man that pulled at my memory. He was a tall, rangy figure and he oozed strength from every part of his being.

"There they are, and there he is, my lord," Sarah-Louise motioned to us.

"Are you sure it is him?" the stranger asked her.

"He confirmed it with his own words, liege," she replied reverently.

"Who's he?" Harry whispered to me.

"No idea," I shrugged. "He looks familiar but only in a way like he reminds me of someone I've seen some time before."

I took a step forward, my sword in my hand, down by my side by ready to defend myself if necessary.

"Why have you lycans invaded this town?" I demanded harshly, remembering my lessons from Captain Paulinos. Dogs had to be shown who their masters were.

"Do not talk to me in that tone, vampire scum," the man spat at me.

"I won't let you kill anyone in this range," I ignored his insult. "This is my town, my range and I will defend it from you dogs."

"Actually, this vampire range belongs to Eirwen of Brenaye Forest," Sarah-Louise stopped the man from retorting. "Well, it did until we cleaned shop."

Harry put his hand on my shoulder to restrain me, not that he could have stopped me but his simple touch brought me back from the edge of throwing myself onto them. I could hear the quiet sob from DCI Bach at the mention of Eirwen's name.

"How did you know that she was here?" I asked, my thoughts diverting to how well hidden we believed that we were. "And what did you want with her by coming here?" After all, if these dogs could find Eirwen, what was to stop Chlothar from doing the same?

"I can still smell the reek of her soul," the man hissed. "She was a wanted murderer of lycans and when it was discovered by chance that she was here, we despatched a pack here to hunt her down."

"Okay, so she's gone… that doesn't explain why you have descended en masse," Petra snarled. "When The Comitia discover that you've caused the trouble to humans that you have, they will despatch the best lycan hunters in Europe."

"I don't think that your beloved leaders will give us any grief," he smiled at her. I could see the wolf in his smile and my hackles started itching. "You see, The Comitia are very eager to track down the House of Chlothar, or rather get Lord Chlothar out of his house and we have given them every opportunity to get their wish."

"How?" Harry asked. "Why would attacking Blackpool mean anything to him?"

"Oh it's not Blackpool that he'll feel the loss of, even though he ruled here once," the wolfman replied. "It's the loss of his beloved wife that will bring him out in revenge."

"Not only her death but the torture of his son as well," Sarah-Louise grinned evilly. "And to think that I wanted to date you." She shook her head.

"If you think you're going to get your hands on Alex, you've gotta get through me, bitch!" Petra moved herself in between us.

"Who are you?" I asked. "Why do you hate my former sire so much?"

"My name is Kieran Gestarde."

I felt a tingle run through my body at his name, the same name of the most powerful Alpha Prime lycan that had ever lived.

"My line was almost ended at the hands of the House of Chlothar but we survived and prospered," he sneered at me. "I know of the name Alex Hayden, the hiding name of Alexander of Farrow's Haven, bodyguard and most trusted servant of Chlothar, Lord of Shadowvale and I will wreak my revenge on your House."

"Bring it on then mutt," I hissed, my fangs bared. "I was there at Kiran's death when my mentor Paulinos de Balurac slaughtered him like the mongrel that he was. I was there when your mighty lycan forces attacked the Shadow Castle and were despatched like the puppies that they were. I fear thee not and I will slay thee too."

The air crackled with metamorphic magic and the gathered lycans whined as the man mutated into a wolf. I was transfixed. Never before had I seen such a vision of beauty, of terror. The wolf was huge. Standing on all four paws, he easily stood as tall as my shoulders. Saliva dripped from his jowls as he sniffed the air, his eyes fixing on me.

I raised my sword, ready to defend myself against any sudden leap and I felt my four companions all draw their own weapons in response. The lycans had stood back into crouching positions and I quickly scanned their numbers.

"Guys, there are thirteen of them left, including Kieran," I started. "He's obviously going to go for me, so that leaves twelve between you four."

"I can drop at least three of them before they move," Petra suggested. "I'll ditch my crossbow again straight after as it will be close quarter fighting thereon in."

"I've got a couple of bullets left," Harry added. "So I can take care of a couple more."

"That will leave us with seven," Bill said. "But don't forget Sarah-Louise is an Alpha."

"She's mine!" Vanessa hissed. "She's responsible for Eirwen's death so I'm going to kill her."

"Let's get to it then," I said. "Petra, Harry, let's not wait for them to attack. Take out your targets and then we charge."

"On three?" Petra nodded at Harry.

The silent three seconds ended with an eruption of noise. Three of the lycans were catapulted backwards by the force of Petra's crossbow while two more dropped, blood oozing from bullet holes in their heads as a testament to Harry's accuracy.

The remaining six jumped. Bill, Petra and Harry took two each and their blades shone in the moon's rays as they fought to keep the lycans out of claws reach.

DCI Bach circled Sarah-Louise, the pair of alpha females eyeing each other cautiously before the wolf leapt at the policewoman. I half saw Vanessa as she parried a claw swipe on her blade before I turned back to face the new Alpha Prime.

I sensed his frustration at the way that my companions were killing off the lesser wolves. I figured that he'd wanted to have me watch my friends die, or get injured, to affect my own confidence. Instead, their fight gave me strength. I sized up the distance between the two of us and took a step forwards, placing myself between him and my friends, just in case he decided to try to despatch one of them before turning his attention to me.

"Come on then, mongel," I snarled. "Let's bring it on and end this."

His response was a loud, low growl and he crept forwards slowly, each step a steady, sure paw as we closed the gap between us. I felt a trickle of fear run through my body as I read the evil look in his eyes, still showing his full human intelligence. Then instinct saved my life. I ducked down and thrust my sword upwards, slicing through the belly of a lycan who had broken free of the main group to attack me from behind.

I shook red blood from my hair as I was showered by the entrails of the lycan before it fell limply to the ground. It didn't even twitch in death, thanks to the precision of my cut. I turned back to Gestarde.

"Just like a lycan to have no honour in battle," I hissed at him. "Always sneaking up from behind, afraid to face your opponent head on. You wonder why the rest of our world despises you?"

He leapt at me. His size had hidden his speed. I found myself dodging to the side just in time as fangs snapped mere inches from my face. I turned quickly to see him already in mid-air, having landed and turned back. I brought up Venenum Draconum, catching his front claws on the edge of the blade. I nearly dropped my sword as the shock of the impact jarred along my arms.

I swayed to the side as Gestarde swiped at me, lashing out with my sword and catching the wolf on the side. However, my blade was simply brushed off despite its magical properties which caught me off balance and pain erupted down my left side. I glanced down to see three deep cuts from the claws of Gestarde and I dodged once more as his fangs bit down on fresh air where my head had been an instant before.

I cast a quick glance at my companions to see them all still standing, but all still engaged in their own battles. Harry looked to be hard pressed but was still keeping his own lycan at arm's length with his dirk. Vanessa and Sarah-Louise were facing each other off, both of them bleeding from wounds they had inflicted on each other.

Any thoughts that I had about helping any of them were quickly shut down as Gestarde leapt at me once again. I found myself backing up, retreating step by step as the strength of the beast threatened to overwhelm me.

I had to rely on my speed and instinct several times just to remain alive, let alone try to get an advantage in the fight and I could sense the pleasure spilling out of the Alpha Prime wolf as he realised just how outclassed I was.

I thrust forwards with my sword, hoping, praying that I would find a soft part of his flesh only to see my blade turned away once more. I felt a touch in my mind, a familiar yet distant memory of an age long past and foresight came to me.

"You're frigging magic resistant," I hissed at the wolf.

I could see the hint of a lupine smile on his jaw and he lunged forward again. I reversed the grip on my sword and smashed the pummel into his face, gaining a satisfying painful yelp from Gestarde before I dropped my sword and went back to my tried and trusted method of fighting; claws and fangs.

I jumped onto the beast's back, raking my nails through the deep, heavy coat of fur and found flesh. I felt the slice of my claws cut into the back of Gestarde and he howled in pain before shaking me loose. My back hit a nearby tree stump, sending an electric shock of pain up my spine and I rolled to the side just as the wolf's teeth bit into the wooden trunk.

I crouched low as he turned back towards me and, as if we were in a synchronised move, we met each other in mid-jump. I grabbed hold of the beast's neck and with my incisors lengthened, I bit down into flesh. Pain erupted through my senses, both empathic as Gestarde felt my fangs pierce his skin and my own pain receptors as his teeth bit into my side.

I hung on to his body as we hit the ground, rolling over each other and I could feel the wash of blood over my mouth. I tasted power as I drank from the vein that I had found and strength returned to my body. Claws raked my legs and back as Gestarde changed his strategy from overpowering me to one of escape.

I could sense his shock and surprise as he realised that I had him in a death grip, my teeth draining his life from his body as I continued to empty his body of blood. My own strength was growing and as quickly as the wolf was ripping into my flesh with his claws, my healing abilities cured me, sealing the cuts and numbing the pain.

The taste of his blood changed and I pulled my mouth away from his body. Spitting the last mouthful to the ground, I looked over the twitching body of the wolf, my claws ready to defend myself. The air crackled as his body seemed to shimmer. The wolf's body was replaced by that of a human, but unlike the confident, rangy figure that had walked into the clearing, Gestarde's body was limp and frail. His throat showed my bite marks and his chest had claw marks where I had gripped his body.

"You'll never win," he gasped. "Even with my death, another will take my place."

"I'm not in a war with you, don't you get that?" I hissed. "I just wanted to be left alone to end my days but you had to come and interfere." I picked up my sword and raised it above my head. "You shouldn't have killed Eirwen."

My blade sliced easily through human bone as I decapitated the lycan Alpha Prime. I caught a feeling of pride and ecstasy rushing through the clearing which almost knocked me from my feet but, as I turned, I saw that my companions were still engaged in battle. I was just about to leap into the fray when all the lycans suddenly dropped to the floor, changing back to their human forms.

"What's happening?" Harry asked as he looked at the man in front of him who was clutching at his head.

"A lycan feels its alpha's death and if that bloke was the big shot alpha, then they'll be hurting all the more," Petra smiled. Before anyone could stop her, she rammed her dirk into the chest of the woman on her knees in front of her.

"Petra! Stop!" Harry cried out.

"No Harry, Petra is right." Bill said. "Even though they're back in human form, they are still werewolves and they will kill again."

"I'll do it," I said softly as Harry's eyes betrayed his reluctance to accept the cold blooded murder that we had to inflict. Even as he opened his mouth to argue, I sliced the neck of his opponent, ending his life.

I watched as Bill and Petra finished off the remaining two lycans before we turned to the DCI. She was standing in front of Sarah-Louise Norris, now back in human form and on her knees. Her chocolate brown eyes found mine and I could sense the pleading from her. Touching her mind quickly, I could feel the love that she had for her brother, the reluctance to have turned him before tonight's battle and the affection for me that she had buried in her heart.

"This has to end," I told her. "You've killed humans for no reason other than your own selfish pride."

"Find Jake a good home," she whispered before the DCI swung her short blade.

I watched as her head rolled to the side, Harry's gasp of shock ringing in my ears and I knew that the way that he looked at me would be changed forever.

Michael Andrews

Chapter Sixteen

"What are we going to do about all the bodies?" Harry asked as he struggled to regain his composure. "I mean, we can't just leave them here."

"I'll make a call," Bill suggested. "The Comitia will take care of it."

"I need to be gone from here before they get here," I said, wiping my sword on my hoodie. I could wash the blood out of the material later, but I needed to clean the blade before it stained. I frowned as I noticed a nick in the edge. I was going to have to find a new whetstone as I had lost mine when I was in New Orleans a few decades before.

"Don't worry. They already know you're here," Petra sighed. She shrugged as she looked at her uncle. "I had to give them a full report after the van Hightinger battle. I told them how you'd helped kill Beddows and his cronies and they agreed that as you'd also left the House of Chlothar, that you were to be monitored, not killed."

"Thanks… I think," I chuckled. "Make your call Bill and then head back to Y'cart's. I need to go and keep a promise."

I walked over to where Sarah-Louise's body lay on the floor. I saw a silver necklace around her throat and reached down and unfastened it. There was a pendant attached but out of respect, I resisted the urge to open it, despite the prickle that I felt when I held it. I launched myself into the air and within minutes, I settled onto the roof of Detective Jackson's house.

I could hear the cries of a baby and tried to tune it out as I floated down towards the guest bedroom window. Reaching out with my mind, I sensed the worry emanating from the room and I tapped the window quietly. The curtains were pulled back and I was face to face with a wide eyed Jake. He quickly opened the window and ushered me inside.

"That looked so cool... you floating there like that," he giggled. "Will you take me flying?"

"Sure Jake, I promise." I handed him the pendant which he took, his expression turning sombre.

"Are they all dead?" he asked quietly.

"I'm afraid so. Your parents were killed in the initial fight but Sarah-Louise remained to the end. She asked us to make sure that you were looked after when she realised that she was going to die." I tried to make it sound comforting, despite my hatred of their kind.

"I guess that she was okay as a sister but she... they were werewolves and killed people," he snarled. He turned to the bedside table and opened the drawer. He pulled out a hammer. "I got this from Mr Jackson's tool box that was in his car."

"What are you going to do with it?"

"She told me that the crystal inside the pendant carried a spell which I could use to kill you," Jake replied.

I backed up as he opened the locket and a small diamond fell into his palm. My hairs stood on end as dark arcane power rippled across the room. I felt a twinge of pain as it touched me and couldn't help but let out a small gasp as my nerve endings began to complain under the magic assault. Jake looked up from the diamond which was glowing a deep red.

"Shit, sorry mate," he stammered out and placed the diamond on the table. Before I could warn him about the magical power, he brought the hammer down, smashing the crystal into a powder. My pain stopped immediately.

"How?" I asked in amazement, expecting my young friend to have felt a backlash from destroying a mage's spell.

"Sarah-Louise said that I was going to be the next Alpha Prime because of my magical resistance," Jake shrugged. "I thought she was talking about the Transformers or something but it makes sense now."

"You're going to be an Alpha Prime?" I stuttered, backing away slightly. I saw a frown spread over his face.

"What's one of those?" he asked. "I didn't get it and I tried looking it up on my phone."

"An Alpha Prime is like, the leader of the lycans," I explained. "Are you sure that she didn't bite you or anything?"

"Definitely sure," Jake nodded. "I don't want to be a werewolf. I'd prefer to be a vampire."

"No, you wouldn't," I sighed. "Trust me on that."

I studied him for a moment and my senses picked up his sorrow at his parents' death tinged with relief that he wasn't going to be turned into a lycan. I hugged him tightly.

"Stay with Detective Jackson tonight and we'll come by in the morning and sort something out as to who's going to look after you," I said. "Have you got any relatives?"

"No, all my grandparents died ages ago and my folks were only children," he sighed. "I've not got any aunts or uncles."

"Well, don't worry buddy," I reassured him. "I'm friends with DCI Bach and I'm sure we can get you sorted." I glanced at the clock on the bedside table. It wasn't that long until sunrise and I needed to get back to Y'cart's. "I'll swing by tomorrow after the sun goes down."

"So that's really true as well?" Jake asked. "You can't go in the sun?"

"Nope. I'll burn to a frazzle and become a nice barbeque for you," I laughed, bringing a smile back to his face. I offered him my fist, which he bumped and I was gone, out of the window, catching an air current back to Y'cart's.

I landed on the driveway and did away with my glimmer, causing DCI Bach to drop the cigarette that she was smoking. She cursed at me, causing Bill to chuckle as he finished his own rollup before we headed inside the house.

Everyone was sitting in the lounge, pensive faces despite the victory that we had achieved. It was a victory that had come at a high cost.

"How's Jason?" I asked, concerned for the ten year old mischief maker.

"I've still got him sedated," Y'cart replied, rubbing a hand over her brow. Harry put a reassuring hand on her shoulder, and she placed her own on his. That was going to cause me some serious grief, especially now that Eirwen had gone.

"Well, I guess that Gestarde's presence answered my query about what Eirwen told me," I said to no-one in particular. I saw funny looks on the faces of the others and explained how her ghost had visited me earlier in the evening.

"Are you sure that you didn't bang your head in your sleep?" Petra queried. I threw her the look that it deserved.

"She told me that there was a presence behind the pack, someone looking for me so, with the presence of the Alpha Prime, that all points to him," I shrugged. "Talking of which, Jake was being lined up to become the next Prime."

"Are you sure?" Bill asked, suddenly sitting upright.

"Well, that's what he said his sister told him, and he is also resistant to magic," I confirmed. "I saw him smash a crystal that reeked of Auron's magic and he didn't even flinch."

"Who is this Auron?" Vanessa asked. "That's twice you've mentioned him now."

"Auron Robino is the leader of all dark mages," Y'cart explained. "He is evil incarnate. If there was an embodiment of the Devil on Earth, he would be it."

"Didn't you say that you got your sword from him?" Petra nudged me.

"That was when I was the son of Satan," I leaned over to whisper in her ear. She shot me a look of disbelief before Harry started to chuckle having seen the edges of my smile.

"Git!" the blonde huntress huffed.

"We need to sort out someone to take Jake in," I said. "I want him close by if possible so we can keep our eyes on him."

"I've taken care of it," Bill replied, walking back into the room. I hadn't seen him leave.

"What do you mean?" Harry asked. "I think even you couldn't keep up with a thirteen year old lad these days."

I saw Petra and Bill exchange a glance and she stood up from her seat next to me. It was almost as though she was positioning herself in between her uncle and me.

"The Comitia have already picked him up from Detective Jackson's," Bill told us.

"What?" I clenched my fists, restraining myself from flying across the room. "You've given him to those bastards?"

"Listen Alex, I'm sure Bill has a good reason," Harry interrupted me. "At least let him explain."

"Fine. Explain."

"I spoke with a close friend of mine and explained who he was and how important he is," Bill started. "We need to protect him from any lycan who wants to get hold of him."

"He's got a point, Alex," Y'cart added. "With the Alpha Prime dead, they will be looking for new leadership."

"And if he was already marked to become the next Alpha Prime, then it makes sense I guess," I groaned. I rubbed my temples.

"Are you okay, Alex?" asked Harry, concern on his face.

"I don't know. I've got a blinding headache. It's like a mounting pressure on my brain and it's getting worse," I stood but sat down quickly, the room spinning.

"I'll go and get you a glass of water and some herbs that should ease it," Y'cart said. She got up and left for the kitchen while Harry sat by my side.

"So are you okay with the arrangements for Jake?" he asked.

"As long as I can see him every now and then," I replied. "Me and him were becoming friends and I think he'll need friends over the next few years."

"I think that won't be a problem," Bill breathed a sigh of relief. "The couple who are taking him are both trained Comitia members. Julie is an analyst while I trained Chris so he will be able to protect him."

I was just about to answer when a chill ran down my back. I stood, my hand reaching for my sword as Y'cart came through the door, a serious look on her face.

"I'm so sorry, Alexander," she started. "You know that I am unable to refuse him entry."

"Everyone get back behind me," I snarled, putting all of my authority into my voice.

Harry stood by my side, a worried look on his face while Vanessa automatically followed my vampire tone of command. I could sense Bill and Petra torn in indecision but it was too late as a tall, imposing figure followed Y'cart into the room. My mind battled with itself to keep my identity, to keep my individuality and above all, to keep myself alive.

"Who's he?" asked Harry, his voice barely above a whisper as silence descended on the room.

"My name is Paulinos de Balurac, Detective Shepherd," the Captain introduced himself. "I am Captain of the Guard of the Royal House of Shadowvale."

"What is your purpose here, Captain?" Vanessa found her voice.

"I have come for Eirwen Forrester, formerly Eirwen of Brenaye Forest," he replied solemnly.

"My mistress is dead, Captain," Y'cart replied. "She passed at the hands of a lycan pack."

"That I am aware of," the Captain explained. "I was following the hound Gestarde throughout Europe when I found myself back here in Lancastrian territory. I discovered of her murder from a lycan that I trapped."

"So if you know that she is dead, what do you want now?" Harry asked. I almost cursed as he eased himself in front of me but I resisted the urge to pull him aside to protect him.

"I was hunting down her killers when I heard the battle earlier this evening and upon arrival, I saw him." He pointed at me. A shiver ran down my back. "Alexander, our sire misses you deeply and will be greatly relieved to discover that you are alive."

"I'm not going back," I stammered out. "You can kill me, my Captain, but I will never return to the Shadow Castle."

"Look, mate, you heard him," Petra butted in, "and if you have a problem with that, you've got me to deal with."

The Captain studied the blonde hunter for a moment before a smile spread across his face. He turned back to meet my eyes.

"I like her, Alexander," he chuckled. "She's got spirit. Relax your sword hand, my young apprentice, for your death is not foredoomed tonight."

"I hope not," I muttered.

"I saw how you despatched the lycan Gestarde and that will please Lord Chlothar," Paulinos smiled. "I saw that you learned my lessons well and fought him the only way you could."

"With fang and claw!" we both said together.

"With fang and claw, my young friend," he said. He was by my side in an instant, startling the humans in the room and clasped my shoulders. "You fought well and made me very proud. Killing an Alpha Prime is no mean feat and our Household now has two kills to our name."

"I'm not in the Household any longer," I insisted. "Not since our sire tried to kill me." That brought a gasp from Harry and Petra but Y'cart met the glance from the Captain.

"He still does not know the truth, Captain," she explained.

"It is not for me to tell," he replied to her before turning back to me. "I am not here to bring you home; that must be by your own choice."

"Then I'll never return," I smiled, relieved in part that I was still free.

"But I must bear Eirwen back to our sire," Paulinos said. "I will take her home."

We walked upstairs, Y'cart and Harry following and opened the bedroom door leading to Eirwen's body. I heard Y'cart sniffle before an agonised cry from the room next door.

"I need to replenish Jason's potion," Y'cart stopped. "I'll be right back."

She turned and Harry followed her back downstairs.

"Who is Jason and what ails him?" Paulinos queried.

"He was bonded to Eirwen and his mind is collapsing." I felt a tear escape my eye which I quickly wiped away. It wouldn't do well to show weakness in front of the Captain. We turned and entered Jason's room. I stepped over to him to lay a hand on his forehead. He was covered in sweat and his body was shaking.

"His mind cannot cope with the death of his bonded vampire," Paulinos told me.

"I know. He's only ten," I replied sadly. "Eirwen bonded him to save his life. Now with her death, he will follow."

"It would be merciful to end it now," the Captain told me. "If you cannot do it, I will make it quick. A boy should not suffer such an agonizing death."

"I will not kill him," I snapped. "If we can release his bond, he will recover."

"Then do it. Remove Eirwen's touch from his mind."

"I don't have the power," I snapped back at him. "I was never shown." I studied my former tutor for a moment. "But you can, can't you?"

"Ah, now we have a problem," he smiled at me. It wasn't a pleasant smile. "You need something that only I can give but what will I receive in return?"

I could feel the noose tightening around my neck.

"Is Connor still alive?" I asked suddenly.

"Connor?   Ah yes, the connection with Detective Shepherd runs strong within our problem," Paulinos sighed. "It is strange that he and you should find each other after his son joined our House."

"Has he turned?"

"He would be dead if he hadn't, you know that from experience."

I remembered the excruciating pain of my body's conversion to vampirism and nodded, knowing that if he still lived, Connor would have fed on human blood within weeks of being bitten by Chlothar.

"I offer a trade," I started. "Release Jason from Eirwen's bond and allow Connor to come home and I will return to the House."

"That deal is not for me to make, my young friend," Paulinos explained.   "Releasing a member of the Household is the choice of both the Lord and the individual."

"Then take my offer to Lord Chlothar," I said. "Tell him that I will be willing to return to my former position if Connor is freed to come back to his father."

"I will convey your message, but I fear that Connor will not leave willingly," the Captain replied. "He has taken to his new life wholeheartedly."

"Can you at least try?" I begged. "His father loves him dearly and misses him greatly."

"Trust me," he patted my shoulder. "As a sign of faith," he started before placing a hand on Jason's brow.

I tensed, thinking that he would harm my little friend but the look of painless relief that spread over the unconscious lad's face told me that the Captain had removed the bonding.   Y'cart and Harry came racing back into the room, stopping as Jason's eyes flickered open.

"Mummy? Daddy?" he cried out, sitting up, rubbing his eyes.

"They're at home buddy," Harry knelt by his side. "You've been poorly and Auntie Y'cart has been looking after you."

"Am I better now?" the lad asked.

"You sure are," I told him. "Thank you," I nodded to the Captain.

We left Harry with Jason, while Y'cart fetched Vanessa to call his parents and we stood in the doorway of Eirwen's room. I felt regret flowing from his body and I placed a hand on the Captain's arm.

"You loved her as well?" I finally realised why he had never taken a lover in the eight hundred years that I'd known him.

"She was never going to be mine, so I admired her from afar," he sighed. "I need to depart."

"Will you tell Lord Chlothar of my presence here?" I asked.

"If you want me to make the offer, then he must know that you are alive. He will torture the information from me one way or another if I do not tell him your location."

"So I've either got to move on again or allow him to capture me," I sighed.

"You're not going anywhere," Harry interrupted us.

"But…"

"But nothing Alex," he stated. "You deserve a chance to have a stable home and somewhere to rest up. I'd like that to be with me."

My eyes locked with the Captain's for a moment, the unspoken question answered with a barely perceivable nod. I felt a little piece of my humanity lost in that moment as I promised not to tell Harry about Connor and to withdraw my offer of exchange.

"Your presence here will not be reported to our Sire," the Captain said. "Take care Alexander, for I sense further trials ahead of you."

To Harry's eyes, a blur sped from the room, out of the window but to mine, I watched as he lovingly picked up Eirwen's body, raised a hand in farewell and flew out of the window.

"Come on, let's go back down to the others," Harry smiled at me. I allowed him to lead the way, closing off the pain of betrayal in my heart.

Epilogue

"Come on Alex, wake up already!" Jason's voice echoed around my bedroom.

"Argh, what are you doing in here?" I groused.

I pulled open the drapes around my bed to see that it was only a quarter to four. Jason was bouncing around my room wearing a hideous looking jumper with a red nosed reindeer and elves woven into it. I had to fight to hold back a giggle.

"The sun hasn't gone down yet," I moaned. "Let me sleep for another hour!"

"But it's Christmas!" he shouted at the top of his voice. "I wanna open my pressies!"

"Looks like you're already wearing the best one," I chuckled. He stopped bouncing, his face screwing up into a scowl.

"Auntie Nessie got me this," he groaned. "She knitted it herself!"

"Don't let her hear you calling her Nessie," I warned. "Unless you want to stand up at the dinner table."

I saw him grab hold of his bottom and look around. Breathing a sigh of relief that the door was closed, he jumped as I used his distraction to blur out of bed and grab him into a tickle. He soon called 'uncle' and he left me to get ready.

Now, I know that people think that vampires are unholy so why would they celebrate Christmas, but most of us weren't born until after the Common Era began and Christianity had spread throughout Europe. Besides, who doesn't like getting presents?

I headed downstairs, grabbed a strong cup of coffee and headed into the lounge. Everyone was there. Well, everyone except Eirwen of course. In a way, it was nice. It was my first proper Christmas in a century and a half, and my first family Christmas in so much longer.

Presents were exchanged, Jason being very excited about the black cape that I had got him. Of course, the fake vampire fangs were a secondary present. I even stretched my goodwill cheer to getting Petra a set of silver throwing daggers. However, my goodwill spirit was tested as she thanked me underneath the mistletoe later after she had drunk a couple of eggnogs too many!

Finally, after a huge turkey dinner, we bade goodbye to everyone and it was just Harry, Y'cart and me. I could feel worry mixed with affection flowing from the pair of them so, as we sat down, I nodded at them to tell me the news that I had already been expecting.

"Alex, now that Eirwen has gone, there isn't really much left for me," the witch started. "I have been with my mistress for almost a millennia but now I need to think about what is best for me."

"What is best for you is to get with Harry," I interrupted. "Harry, it's time for you to think about yourself as well. However, what about the longevity issue?"

"Y'cart was explaining that to me," Harry replied. "Short of me becoming a warlock…" I shot him a frown. "There is only one other alternative."

"I am going to give up my power," Y'cart said.

My mouth dropped open.

"But that means you'll be defenceless," I argued. "No matter what the Captain promised, I fully expect Chlothar to come for us."

"I trust the Captain's word," she argued. "And even if I didn't, it wouldn't matter. I love Harry and we are going to be a couple."

"Plus, she still has all of her knowledge and experience," Harry added.

"And I can still mix potions," Y'cart smiled.

"It's your decision," I shrugged, secretly pleased that she was willing to make such a sacrifice for Harry. Of course, this left me with a dilemma. A new relationship is only for two, not three.

I stood up and hugged the pair, before starting for the door.

"Where are you going?" Harry asked.

"I was going to go out on a scout around," I replied. "I need to start looking for somewhere to go."

"Don't be stupid," Y'cart chuckled. "Do you really think that Harry would let you just up and leave, let alone the promise that I made to Eirwen."

"You're staying put, kiddo," Harry hugged me.

"Besides, I have something for you." Y'cart reached over and pulled out an envelope. It was post stamped from the USA. "Eirwen had been looking into something but now she isn't here, I thought that you would want this… just in case."

"Just in case of what?" I asked, reaching out with slightly shaking hands. Eirwen had always kept quiet whenever I asked her about her trips to the US and I thought that she had taken that secret to her grave. Now, was the answer in my hands?

I opened the envelope and pulled out some sheets of parchment. I frowned.

"It's in Latin!" I grumbled. "I can't read Latin."

"Oh my… there is something that Alexander the Great can't do," the witch laughed, while Harry went to ruffle my hair. I pulled back automatically but he still managed to mess up my blonde locks.

"So what is it? What does it say?" I begged. "I know you can read it."

Y'cart looked at me, her expression turning pensive.

"Eirwen, like you, had become tired of living forever. Instead of going for a sunwalk, she decided to do something different. What you have in your hands is the cure to the curse."

"The cure to what curse?" I asked.

"According to lore, the very first vampire was a preacher who was cursed by a combination of the witch he loved and betrayed and the Church whose rules and laws he broke. What you hold in your hands, Alexander, is the curse breaker. The way for a vampire to become human once more."

THE END

Alex Hayden will return in "The Cauldron of Fire."

ABOUT THE AUTHOR

Michael Andrews is a Birmingham based author and
poet whose debut novel 'For The Lost Soul' has
become an international seller.
'The Empty Chair' shows his passion for trying to
help solve the issue of bullying and is his second book
released, supporting the UK Charity BeatBullying.org.
'Under A Blood Moon' and 'The Howling Wind' are
the first two books in The Alex Hayden Chronicles,
his new paranormal series.

Printed in Great Britain
by Amazon

83817677R00103